Stained Heart

A Novel

By Crystal Joy

Author of *Completely Captivated, Completely Yours, Shackled Heart,* and *Shattered Heart*

Edited by: Lost Canyon Editing
Cover design by: Lyndsey Lewellen

For Jen—my dearest lifelong friend. I'm so blessed to have someone as special and supportive as you by my side.

Stained hearts love
in the deepest shades
of red!
♡

XOXO,

Crystal Jay

Table of Contents

Prologue

LIEUTENANT COLONEL CALEB Meyers squinted through his night-vision goggles. The dust storm blanketed every inch of the sky, concealing the moon completely. He gripped the controls of the helicopter and accelerated off the landing zone.

Behind him, the wounded solider they'd just rescued let out a loud painful scream. The two pararescuemen yelled instructions to each other over the roar of the helicopter as they provided medical treatment to the double-amputee.

Caleb glanced at his copilot. "It never gets any easier. Hearing their screams, I mean."

"No, it doesn't. When we get home, I'll still be able to hear them. In my dreams, anyway." Captain Seth Seymour sat rigid in his seat. His pointer finger tapped against his thigh, and his gaze remained focused on the sky. "I can't believe this is it. Our last mission."

"It hasn't hit me yet." Caleb scrubbed a hand over his face. "It'll sink in when the night is over. The storm has gotten worse since we first took off." His grip tightened on the controls. "I've never flown in conditions this bad. I can't see anything."

Seth gave a forced laugh. "Stop being such a wuss, Meyers."

His friend's attempt to calm his nerves didn't work. Not when Seth was just as nervous as he was. Seth never could hide much from him. After becoming friends in high school, then spending the last decade in the air force together, he could probably read Seth better than anybody.

Static buzzed from the radio before the pilot of the trailing aircraft spoke. "Confirm that you are in a left-hand turn."

"A left-hand turn?" Caleb glanced at his instruments.

Seth cursed under his breath. "He must be disoriented."

Panic seized Caleb's insides. If the other pilot veered their way and collided with their aircraft, they'd all end up … He stopped his thoughts. He needed to stay focused and get them all to safety. But the complete darkness was messing with his head too. Which way was up, and which way was down? Out of the corner of his eye, a green blob shot past.

"That's the trail aircraft. They almost crashed into us because we're going too slow!" Seth yelled.

His heart pounded hard and fast. He couldn't see

much of anything. How was he supposed to fly them to safety?

"Meyers? Are you okay?"

Caleb sat frozen in place. His head swam and waves of nausea rolled through his stomach.

Seth maintained control of the aircraft and gave instructions to the wingman for independent recovery back to the base.

But then, the aircraft jolted to the left. Bullets sliced through the fuselage. One sizzled past his head, nicking the tip of his ear.

Seth's blood-curdling scream pierced through the roaring chaos.

Caleb shot a look in his direction. A red stain extended from Seth's rib cage like a ripple in the water.

His eyes widened. *I have to do something.*

He took over the controls and accelerated to a higher altitude. They had to get out of enemy fire. He yelled to the men in back. "Seth's been hit. I need a PJ."

One of the pararescuemen dove through the narrow passageway to the cockpit and leaned over Seth. A loud groan escaped through Seth's clenched teeth.

Guilt ripped through his chest. "I'm sorry. This was my fault. I got too focused on the mission. I didn't correctly evaluate the threat."

"No. Don't say that. Don't you dare apologize to me." Seth's voice sounded strained and faint. His eyelids fluttered open and closed as he went in and out of consciousness. "I'm the one who's sorry, for so much …"

Sorry? Why was Seth sorry? Now wasn't the time to ask. He needed to get the entire crew to safety. All of their lives depended on him.

Chapter 1

G RACE CUNNINGHAM STEERED her car off the
highway as Maple Valley's water tower emerged
over the top of a familiar paint-chipped barn. Her
stomach coiled into tight knots. *This was a bad idea.* She
should turn around and go home.

No one expected her to attend the wake, except for
Amanda. Last week, Grace's friend had called to share
the news: Seth Seymour had died during his last
deployment in Iraq.

Even though they hadn't spoken in years, his death
brought an unexpected ache at the loss of his life, and the
desire to pay her respects to his family, who had lived
next door.

She frowned. If only paying respects to her childhood
friend didn't include visiting her hometown.

She shook away the encroaching memories and
turned on to Ashmend Road. In eleven years, not much
had changed. Streetlamps lined the uneven redbrick
road. The letter *C* still hung lopsided outside of Candy

Galore. Val's Diner had the same blue paint scrolled across the window, advertising an All You Can Eat Buffet on Saturdays. A worn, white truck was parked diagonally in front of The Joint. No doubt Calvin Kraus sat at the bar with two glasses of whiskey and a mouthful of stories about the good ol' days on the farm.

Grace almost smiled, but it quickly faded as she pulled into the last empty parking spot in front of Resting Haven Funeral Home. She leaned back in her seat and chewed on her thumbnail.

Too bad Amanda wasn't here. But her friend was on a month-long trip in Greece with her hunky boyfriend and wouldn't be back for another week.

She bit down harder on her thumbnail, causing it to bleed. Could she really go inside and face all the people she'd left behind?

She reached for her purse in the passenger's seat, pulled out travel-sized tissues, and wrapped one around her thumb. Truth be told, she wasn't *that* concerned about seeing most people. Just one person.

Caleb Meyers. According to Amanda, her twin brother, Caleb, had left the air force and moved back to Maple Valley for good.

Grace closed her eyes and inhaled slowly. Maybe she wouldn't see him at the wake. Maybe he'd already come and gone. If she could make it out of here without seeing her ex-boyfriend, she'd be able to relax.

Caleb probably hated her, and she didn't blame him. She'd broken up with him when she'd moved away eleven years ago. She left without saying goodbye, without giving him an explanation.

But back then, she hadn't been ready to tell him the truth.

A steady stream of people strolled out of the funeral home, heading toward their vehicles. She sank lower in her seat, then sat up straight, shaking her head in disgust. This was ridiculous. *She* was ridiculous. She wasn't a helpless little girl anymore, cowering in a corner, hiding from her fears. She was a grown woman who'd risen above her circumstances.

And besides, today, she and Caleb didn't matter. This was about paying respects to an old friend who had lost his life far too early.

She pulled back her shoulders and straightened the wrinkles on her black dress. She didn't come all this way just to hide in her car. She was done hiding.

She smoothed her hair and stepped out of her car, then strode toward the funeral home. *This is for you, Seth.*

❦

CALEB TENSED AS he stepped into the crowded chapel of Resting Haven Funeral Home. The long line curved around the room, stopping near the far corner where

Seth's mom, dad, and sisters stood. The bright fluorescent lights illuminated their red-rimmed eyes and pale tear-stained cheeks as they accepted condolences from friends and family.

Heat rose up the back of his neck. Did they understand how sorry he was? If he could go back in time, he'd change the way he reacted that night. He wouldn't panic. He would assess the threat correctly so Seth wouldn't get shot.

Seth's mother glanced his way. Had they told her Seth bled out before reaching the hospital? The bloodstain on his friend's shirt had grown and deepened while Seth's body had paled and slackened.

Caleb adjusted the knot in his tie, loosening it as his gaze drifted to the urn. He'd give anything to see Seth one more time, to give his friend a proper goodbye. To ask him why he'd apologized. It still didn't make sense. Seth had taken control of the aircraft and kept them from crashing. What would he be sorry for?

Behind him, Sandy Johnson sniffled. He reached for a box of Kleenex on an end table and handed it to her.

"Thanks." Sandy blew her nose, sounding like a foghorn. "I can't stop crying. Thirty is too young to go." She blew her nose again and sent Caleb a sad smile that deepened the crow's-feet around her hazel eyes. "I remember when you and Seth would ride your skateboards all over town. You used to do those fancy tricks on the curb, and Seth would jump and flip his skate-board in the air. You two were quite the duo back in the day." Her rouge-colored cheeks darkened to bright red. "Don't mind my blubbering. I don't want to make this any harder on you."

He put his arm around Sandy's shoulders, giving her a side hug. "It's okay."

Besides his dad and sister, Sandy was one of the people he'd missed most during deployments. She had an infectious laugh that made it impossible not to join in. When he'd moved back and walked into Candy Galore, her jaw had dropped. She did something she'd never done before. She ran to him and wrapped her arms around his waist. The scents of homemade chocolate and peppermint rising from her apron reminded him of younger days and buying sweets with his allowance.

Sandy crumpled the tissue in her hands, and a look of concern spread across her weathered face. "How are *you* doing?"

He stiffened. "I'm still in shock, I guess."

People asked him that question a lot lately, and he never knew how to answer. Depending on the day, his emotions ranged from angry, sad, depressed, all the way to guilty. Guilt, especially, seemed to be at the forefront of his emotions, crawling around his insides until he no longer felt comfortable in his own skin.

Survivor's guilt. Other guys from the air force had

talked about it, but he had never experienced it until he'd lost Seth. It would probably do him good to talk to someone. But how was he supposed to get over the fact that he could've prevented his best friend from dying?

He tugged on his shirt collar as the line moved near a long table displaying pictures of Seth at various ages: Seth standing outside of Maple Valley Elementary School with a gap-toothed grin, camping with his Boy Scout troop, pitching during a baseball state championship game, smoking cigars with Caleb after one of their missions.

He pinched the bridge of his nose. He would not let his emotions get to him. Not here in front of all these people.

Sandy tapped on his shoulder. "The family is waiting for you, dear."

Caleb glanced up from the photos. Sue, Doug, Becky, and Lauren looked at him expectantly. He lifted his chin and moved forward. "I'm sorry for your loss." Those words weren't enough to make up for Seth's absence, but now that he was standing in front of the Seymours, his mind had gone blank.

Sue wrapped him in a hug, enveloping him in a cloud of flowery perfume. "Seth was lucky to have a best friend like you."

"If there is anything you need, please let me know."

Her lips quivered. "I have something for you." She

picked up a cardboard box and handed it to him. "These are some of Seth's things. He would've wanted you to have them."

His lungs constricted, making it difficult to breathe. "Thank you." He kissed her cheek, tucked the box beneath his arm, and strode quickly out of the chapel. He needed fresh air. He needed to get away from all these people who would never understand the turmoil he held within.

❧

GRACE SHIFTED HER weight from one foot to the next. *Ugh*, her feet already ached. What had she been thinking wearing her high heels to a wake? She should've worn her dressy flats.

She hadn't even made it inside the funeral home yet. Every time she opened the door, someone else walked out and recognize her, including Kendall Frasier, one of her friends from high school.

"Hold on, Jeffrey, Mommy's talking." Kendall blew bangs from her eyes. She reached for her toddler's hand, then tugged him closer to her side.

Grace smiled. In a few years, Kendall would miss these days. She certainly did. As a busy single mom trying to balance motherhood, school, and work, her son's first few years had flown by in a blur; his first babbles and giggles now only sweet memories.

"Sorry, what was I saying?" Kendall picked up Jeffrey and rested him on her hip. "Oh yeah, where do you live now?"

"Orick Hills. I moved there a year ago and opened a bed-and-breakfast with my mom."

"Wow. That's exciting."

Grace withheld a sigh. When her mom had asked if she wanted to co-own a bed-and-breakfast, she had happily accepted. She'd quit her full-time job as a social worker and dove headfirst into managing Cedar Crest. Having flexible hours, working from home, and getting to spend more time with her son seemed like a win-win.

What she hadn't accounted for was how much physical work would be needed—repainting, refurnishing, cleaning, maintenance. The small amount of sales they'd earned went straight to repair costs. Bottom line: they needed more guests.

Jeffrey squirmed in Kendall's arms. "I better get him down for a nap. Take care."

"You too." As Grace waved goodbye, she turned to face the worn, brick building. One of the double doors creaked open, and she took a step back. Her breath caught in her throat.

Caleb.

Her heart wobbled as she eyed him up and down. Thick blond hair that had once draped loosely over his forehead was gone, replaced with a short, tousled style highlighted by the sun. His dark suit coat fit snugly around his broad shoulders, and his black tie accentuated the intensity in his sky-blue eyes. Heat flushed beneath her cheeks. *Wow.* Twenty-nine sure looked good on him.

"Grace?"

It was just her name, but a mixture of emotions seeped through his short response. Surprise. Curiosity. Irritation. "What are you doing here?"

"Your sister called and told me about Seth. I came to pay my respects."

He opened his mouth, then closed it. His chin jutted out slightly and his jaw noticeably tightened.

Grace tucked a strand of hair behind her ear. She had the overwhelming urge to tell him why she hadn't said goodbye to him all those years ago, but now was not the time or place.

He adjusted the cardboard box in his hands.

"What's in the box?" she asked.

"I don't know. Seth's mom just gave it to me. It has some of his things."

"I'm sure you miss him a lot."

Caleb nodded.

She adjusted the purse strap over her shoulder. "The wake is almost over. I should get going."

"Yeah, me too." He scrubbed a hand over his clean-shaven face. "I need to get to work."

She should end the conversation and go inside, but

curiosity won, and she had to ask. "Where do you work?"

"At Riverside Fire Station. I'm a firefighter."

"Oh. You haven't been back for that long. How are you already a firefighter?" The second she asked, she pressed her lips together. Now he knew she'd talked to Amanda about him.

"I trained while I was overseas. I figured I'd want a backup eventually."

Her eyebrows lifted. How impressive that he'd trained to become a firefighter while also being a full-time pilot. That couldn't have been easy to do both.

"Well …" He scratched behind his head. "Take care."

Relief flooded through her as he turned to go; and yet, the short conversation had left many things unsaid. "Caleb?"

He faced her, his sky-blue eyes meeting her gaze. "Yeah?"

"I'm sorry. For not saying goodbye to you before I moved. I wish I had."

He put two fingers up to his forehead in a polite salute. Before he turned, it almost looked like he smiled, but he turned too fast for her to be certain.

As she watched him walk away, the weight of their past hung over her. What would have happened if she'd stayed in Maple Valley? What would he have said if she'd told him she was pregnant?

Chapter 2

GRACE STACKED THE pile of bills on the table, setting them next to her laptop. She picked up each one and recorded the costs in an Excel spreadsheet. Their financial situation was as somber as the wake had been one week prior.

Mom reached for the bills that Grace had already entered and glanced at the first few before tossing them aside. "We'll never make a profit at this rate. How did you let me talk you into this?"

Grace stopped typing. "We're a good team, that's how."

Mom perched on the edge of her chair and toyed with her diamond-studded earrings. "Has the water dried up yet?"

"Almost. I pulled up the edge of the carpet in my room and put the fan by it." Yesterday, they'd woken to water seeping into their basement apartment. Too much calcium buildup in the old water heater. They bought a brand-new one to fix the issue, causing their monthly costs to exceed their sales.

Anxious tension weighed heavily on her chest. If they didn't bring in more guests, they couldn't afford to keep Cedar Crest open much longer.

Outside, thunder boomed and shook the old windows. Grace glanced up as a flash of lightning shot across the sky, highlighting the pouring rain.

An unsettled feeling anchored in her gut. How much more water could the levee hold before it broke? If it did, Maple Valley and several other river towns were in the path of the destructive flood. The damage would be extensive.

At least she wouldn't be adding flood damage to her list of costs for the bed-and-breakfast. Thankfully, Orick Hills was far enough from the river that flooding wasn't a threat.

But what about Amanda? She'd just arrived home after her trip to Greece.

Grace should call her friend and convince her to stay somewhere safe, and take her brother, boyfriend, and dad with her. But they all had a stake in Maple Valley. None of them would want to leave. Maybe the levee would hold.

Grace picked up another bill. Or maybe they would get trapped in their homes or businesses when the water rushed in.

She glanced at Mom above the laptop screen. She

was becoming more and more like her every day. A worrywart. A fussbudget. Concerning herself with things she couldn't control, like the weather, as if each concern could protect people from getting hurt. Unfortunately, life had a way of reminding her that *that* wasn't true at all.

The kitchen door swung open as Liam trudged into the room wearing his baseball mitt. Beneath the bill of his hat, his glasses slid down his nose. Pushing them up, he let out an exaggerated *huff.* "How am I supposed to practice when it rains all the time?"

"It won't rain every day. I promise we'll have time to practice before your next game."

His shoulders sagged. "I wish I could go outside this afternoon."

"A wise woman once told me 'patience is a virtue.' I've found the saying to be true." She winked at her mom.

Liam rolled his eyes. "Yeah. Okay. I know the *wise woman* is Grandma."

Mom laughed. "Would you do the wise woman a favor and get some flashlights from downstairs in case the power goes out?"

Frowning, Liam yanked the mitt off his hand. "Sure."

Grace playfully taped the bill of his hat. "Thanks, kiddo."

"Don't call me that. I'm not a baby anymore."

"I'm your mom. You'll always be my baby."

The corners of his mouth held the traces of a smile. He was working hard not to give in as he turned around and left the kitchen.

She turned back to the stack of bills. What had gotten into her sweet boy? He'd developed quite the attitude lately.

It felt like a lifetime ago that she'd been pregnant with him. At first, she'd considered giving him up for adoption. At eighteen, she was scared to be a single mom, afraid that she wasn't enough for him. But the more she considered adoption, the more she couldn't fathom giving him up. Her own father had left when she was five, and Mom had fully embraced her role as a single parent, pathing the way and showing Grace that she could do it too. And with Mom's help, the two of them would raise Liam together.

The bell on the front desk chimed twice.

"Be right there." She saved the newest additions to her Excel file and shut off her computer. Who was here? No guests were scheduled to arrive today. Maybe Mr. and Mrs. Ketelsen had decided to arrive early for their anniversary weekend.

She passed through the dining room and stepped into the open foyer. "What a pleasant surprise."

Amanda dropped her overstuffed purse in front of

the modern brick fireplace. "I had to come see you as soon as we got back. I missed you."

"I missed you too. How was your trip?"

"Greece was amazing. Better than I ever could've imagined." Amanda extended her left hand. Light from the crystal chandelier illuminated the sparkling diamond ring on her finger.

"Oh wow, congratulations!" Grace wrapped Amanda in a hug, her words muffled against her friend's damp sweater. "How did Ethan propose? Tell me everything."

Amanda plopped down on the white leather couch, moving her hands as she spoke. "He suggested we take one last boat ride before we flew back, so we went sailing. We were almost back to shore when I saw my dad and Ethan's whole family standing on the dock. I turned to look at Ethan, confused because all those people were there, and he was already down on one knee holding this little beauty." She wiggled her ring finger.

"How romantic. I'm so happy for you." Grace sat next to her friend, her chest swelling with an odd mixture of emotions—part delight, part jealousy.

When they were teenagers, Amanda had been more interested in sports than boys, while Grace had dated Caleb throughout high school. In the yearbook, they were voted "Most Likely Couple to Get Married." Back then, she hoped her classmates were right. But that dream came crashing down when she got pregnant and moved away before anyone—especially Caleb—could discover that Liam wasn't his.

She patted Amanda's knee. "I'm sure Ray is so excited. He's probably told everyone in Maple Valley by now."

"Oh yeah. And he's already asking when we'll start having kids."

"That sounds like your dad. How's he feeling?" Last year Ray had been diagnosed with lung cancer. As unfortunate as the circumstances were, his treatment brought him to the hospital where Grace had worked as a social worker. Amanda saw Grace during one of Ray's chemo sessions, and they started talking again, reuniting their childhood friendship.

"He's in remission and says he's feeling better than he has in years." Amanda pulled her curly blond strands into a messy bun. "Of course, he jokes with Ethan and tells him that the trip to Greece is what saved him, and not his doctor."

Grace laughed. "That sounds like Ray. It's his way of saying thank you to Ethan for being his oncologist."

"You got that right." Smiling, Amanda picked up her purse and reached inside. "I have something for you." Gum wrappers and receipts fell onto the fluffy gray rug before she pulled out a square box wrapped in gold, shiny paper. "Ethan's Pappous made it."

"What is it?"

"Just open it."

She unwrapped the gold paper, revealing a cedar jewelry box. She opened the top and a tiny ballerina spun in a circle, dancing to "Remember When." A picture was taped to the bottom of the lid—Grace and Amanda, their face-painted cheeks pressed together as they stood beside a stack of pumpkins at the Fall Festival.

She lifted her chin to look at Amanda and say thank you when she noticed a pearl bracelet tucked inside the velvet material below the ballerina. She gently tugged on it and placed it on her upturned palm. An engraved heart hung from the bracelet with *Maid of Honor* scrolled across the center.

Her eyes watered. After ten years of not speaking, she wouldn't have expected Amanda to ask *her*. But then again, they'd spent a lot of time getting reacquainted over the last year. And before the years of separation, they'd been best friends since kindergarten. They spent countless sleepovers dressing up their Barbie and Ken dolls, ordaining the weddings of their dreams. Now, it was all coming true for Amanda.

She looked down at the floor. What was her problem? She should be happy for her friend. Amanda had accepted Grace and Liam into her life with compassion and understanding. Being Amanda's maid of honor was the perfect way to show Amanda how grateful she was for their friendship.

Grinning, she slid the bracelet on her wrist and met Amanda's expectant gaze. "I would be honored."

"I was hoping you'd say that." Amanda clapped in child-like delight. "We've already set the date for June 28th."

"Next June?"

"No, this June."

"Wow, that's fast."

"I know it's only four months away, but we can't wait to move in together and start a family." The excitement in Amanda's big blue eyes faded slightly, replaced with apprehension. "There's one other thing I wanted to tell you."

"What is it?"

Amanda toyed with her engagement ring, twisting it around her finger. "We asked Caleb to be a groomsman."

She crossed her legs and folded her arms over her knee. If Caleb was also in the wedding party, they would spend a lot of time together, and at some point, she'd have to tell him about her son. "Speaking of Caleb … I ran into him at Seth's wake."

"I know. He told me."

"Oh." She tried to keep her tone even as she spoke. "What did he say about it?"

"That you tried to get out of the conversation as quickly as possible."

She blew out an exasperated huff. "He wasn't exactly

Mr. Chatty."

"It's okay. I don't blame you. You were probably worried he'd start asking questions and you didn't want to explain everything there, where anyone could walk by and hear you."

"You know me so well."

"I do." Amanda reached for Grace's hands. "But …"

"There's a 'but'?"

"Sooner or later, you'll have to tell Caleb about Liam. You might as well tell him sooner. Get it off your chest. I'm sure you'll feel better after you do."

"Any chance you want to elope instead?"

Amanda gave her a knowing look. "Absolutely not. Just tell my brother the truth."

"The truth, yeah, I'll start with that." A sour taste filled her mouth. How would he react? Would he be angry? Would he walk away without responding? It was hard to guess. After an entire decade apart, Caleb Meyers was practically a stranger.

❧

CALEB PEERED OUT the window of the fire truck as it sped through Maple Valley. Black smoke rose above Candy Galore, clouding the darkening sky. He bounced his leg up and down. Was Sandy inside her shop, or had she already locked up and left before the fire started?

The truck halted in front of the candy store. He looped his arms through the air-pack attached to his seat, buckled it in front of his waist, and jumped out of the truck.

Beauford Jennings jogged over, yanking his turnout gear on over a navy polo with *Mayor* stitched to the breast pocket. "Several sources saw Sandy leave and lock up two hours ago, so I don't think she's in there."

The tension in Caleb's shoulders loosened slightly.

Jennings glanced at the hose. "You're gonna need a two-and-a-half-inch line."

"Got it." Caleb tugged on the hose, running it back and forth across the sidewalk until there were no kinks left. Satisfied, he glanced up and yelled, "Charge the line!"

A woman wearing a flowery dress and apron ducked beneath the yellow warning tape.

Caleb frowned. Civilians shouldn't be close to burning buildings. "You need to get behind the tape, ma'am."

"I can't find my ten-year-old son." Tears streamed down her flushed cheeks. "I was working at Val's Diner when I saw the smoke. Our house is right behind the candy store, so I ran home to check on him, and he's not there."

He gritted his teeth. She was probably worried for nothing, but nonetheless, he needed to take her seriously, just in case. "Where do you think your son is?"

She twisted the bottom of her apron. "He wants to be a fireman when he grows up. Every time he hears a fire truck, he runs outside to watch it drive by." Her lips quivered. "Once, I had to stop him from chasing the truck down the street."

"Where do you think your son is?" he repeated. The woman needed to stop rambling and focus. A fire doubled in size every minute.

"Inside," she croaked.

Caleb cursed under his breath and rushed to the front of Candy Galore to tell the other firefighters. "Keep a look out for a ten-year-old boy. His mom thinks he might be inside."

"We better get in there fast." Nash, one of the other firefighters, stood beside the door with a Halligan bar gripped in his hand. He lifted it to break open the door. But instead of using it, he paused for a moment, then lowered the tool. "The door's already been busted open."

Caleb followed Nash's gaze. The door was slightly ajar. *Had the missing boy broken in to get a look at the fire?*

Nash discarded the Halligan. "Let's look for anything unusual when we're in there."

Nodding, Caleb followed the other firefighters into the smoky shop. Flames blazed all around them, the tendrils of fire blindingly bright in some areas and casting shadows in others.

He squatted low. Adrenaline pumped through his

veins, causing each of his senses to sharpen. He assessed the building, searching for the source. Flames licked through the kitchen door.

He hustled past the booths and tables and into the back room. Heat consumed the kitchen, searing through his thick gear.

A muffled voice came from somewhere in the back of the room.

Caleb stopped for a moment, listening. Could it be the missing boy? Whoever it was, he had to find the person as soon as possible. In three and a half minutes, heat from a fire could reach 1,100 degrees Fahrenheit at the ceiling. And this person could've been in here much longer already.

"Help." The whimper came from behind the cotton candy machine.

Nash dashed around Caleb and maneuvered through the kitchen. He bent down and disappeared for a moment. Seconds later, he came back into view as he gripped the victim's wrists and dragged the body across the floor—the lowest and safest place inside the building.

As Nash moved past, Caleb recognized Sandy's pink petticoat that she often wore when she worked.

His jaw tightened. *No.* Why had Sandy gone back inside after locking up? Had she run back in after she saw the fire? If she'd inhaled too much smoke, she could … No time for that. Nash had Sandy. Caleb needed to find the source of the fire.

He surveyed the kitchen. Red and orange flames shot out from the oven in the back corner. Caleb braced his feet as he opened the bale on the nozzle to switch on the water. He and the other volunteers held tight, whipping the stream from side to side to smother the fire. They continued spraying until the flames diminished and only smoke and steam remained.

He waved his hand in front of his face, trying to clear away the smoke. How had the fire started? He stepped closer, squinting through his mask. A blackened object rested on the stove top. He leaned over and examined the object. A firework.

His eyes widened. There was only one reason a firework would be inside Candy Galore. Someone had started the fire on purpose.

Leaving the evidence in place, he retreated out of the building. He jogged outside and took off his helmet, then sucked in long breaths of air.

The chief strode across the street and patted Caleb's back. "Good work."

"Thanks. Any news on the woman's son?"

"The kid was standing in the crowd across the street, watching."

"Good, glad he's okay." Caleb put his hands on his hips. "You won't believe this. I found a firework inside."

Jennings cursed and spit a wad of chewing tobacco in

the grass. "I'll call an arson investigator."

"I can stay here and wait to talk to the investigator if you want to get back to the station."

"Great. Call me after you're done."

"Of course." Caleb sank to the ground. Anger simmered beneath his core. Who would set Candy Galore on fire? It was a staple in Maple Valley. The store that families piled into on hot summer days, requesting ice cream sundaes. The place teenagers hung out at during early-outs from school.

It was special to many people in town. His parents had met at Candy Galore when his mom worked there in high school. Caleb had taken Grace there many times. They always sat on the same side of a booth, sharing root beer floats.

Grace. She had some nerve to show up at Seth's wake as if she cared about anyone in Maple Valley. Not that anyone else seemed to have a problem with her appearance. One week later and she was still the talk of the town. How nice it was that she'd come. How she'd grown up to be a beautiful woman.

He couldn't argue with that part. She was even prettier than he remembered. Her hair was much longer now, cascading over her slender shoulders. Paired with her porcelain skin and high cheek bones, she held an air of elegance that seemed to fit her name perfectly.

But behind her good looks lay a cold heart. There

was no excuse for the way she'd broken up with him. She should have had the guts to do it in person. After four years of dating, she'd owed him that much. Her apology at the wake couldn't make up for what she'd done.

Caleb rubbed his temples. It didn't matter anymore. If they hadn't broken up, he wouldn't have joined the air force. The men and women he'd fought with were his extended family. The teamwork and camaraderie were second to none. And his experiences—good and bad— had made him the man he was today.

Everything happens for a reason, Dad often said. He and Grace were never meant to be. It was that simple.

❦

THE NEXT MORNING, Caleb tossed a sandbag on top of the temporary levee. Twenty bags down, hundreds more to go. The wall was as high as his knees and about five feet thick.

He would stay out here all day if he needed to. To keep everyone in Maple Valley safe. To protect the people who lived right by the Mississippi River, like Dad, who owned a riverfront home. Because if the sandbag levee didn't hold up, Dad's house would be one of the first houses hit by the flood.

He bent over and picked up another handful of bags. His lower back muscles ached in protest. On his days off from the fire department, he tried to stay busy by sandbagging or helping his dad at the Canine Palace.

Spending time with Dad was the reason he'd left the air force. Some of his comrades had lost parents while they were overseas, and he couldn't let that happen to him. Even though Dad was in remission now, the cancer had taken a toll on his body: he walked slower than he used to, slept a lot, and took longer to do daily tasks, like getting ready in the morning.

Amanda didn't seem to notice. She'd taken care of him when he had cancer, so she only saw the difference between Dad battling cancer and Dad in recovery. She saw a man on the mend, but Caleb saw a fragile old man who could easily get sick again.

Being home was harder than he'd anticipated, though. In Iraq, he'd worked fourteen- to sixteen-hour days. Now, he had way too much down time, which resulted in too much time to think, mostly about Seth and their last mission together.

A month had passed since that fateful night. His grief had lessened slightly, dulled by the encroaching reality of his friend's absence. One day early on, he'd accidently picked up the phone to call Seth, only to hear a woman answer instead. He'd tried playing video games to pass the time, but the ache in his chest returned, a subtle reminder of the long afternoons they spent playing video games in the barracks in order to forget about the imminent dangers that awaited them.

Beauford Jennings waddled over and patted his shoulder. "You okay?"

"Yeah."

Jennings sent him a knowing look before bending down to grab more sandbags. "You got that weird gleam in your eyes again."

"Mind your own business." He kept his tone light and smiled at the mayor.

"Don't make it sound like you're joking. I know you mean it." Jennings ran a hand over his well-groomed beard. "At some point, you should talk about whatever you're going through."

He kept sandbagging, refusing to turn this into some heart-to-heart conversation. Talking about Dad or Seth wouldn't change anything, so there was no point.

Jennings held his hands up in surrender. "Fine. I'll change the subject. Maria would like to invite the firefighters over for dinner on Saturday."

"Who's cooking dinner?" He smirked. "You or Maria?

"Maria is." Narrowing his eyes, he pointed a pudgy finger at Caleb. "For your information, I only burned lasagna once."

He laughed. "Charred is more like it, but whatever makes you feel better."

Tires crunched along the gravel road. His sister's red

Ford Escort came to a stop, kicking up dust. She stepped out of the car, holding a drink carrier with green smoothies. The sunlight reflected off her engagement ring.

His sister was engaged. His sister was getting married. It still hadn't sunk in.

She placed the smoothies on one of the folding tables and practically skipped over to the volunteers. "Guess what I just did."

"This is a hard one. Did you go to Val's Diner and convince Valerie to make green smoothies again?"

She gave him a playful shove. "Ethan and I bought a house."

His eyebrows raised. "That's great."

"Wait until you see it." She moved her hands as she spoke. "It's move-in ready, which is what we were looking for. With Ethan working so many hours at the hospital and many of my pregnant patients in their third trimesters, we barely have enough time to plan the wedding, much less remodel a house."

He smiled. "Sounds perfect."

"It is. It has four bedrooms upstairs, a master bedroom on the first level, and a finished basement that will make a great playroom."

His lips parted. She was so ready to get married and start a family, while he was still a bachelor. He'd dated on and off in his twenties, but nothing serious. It wouldn't have been fair to make a girlfriend date long-distance, letting her sit at home and worry about his safety.

And now, dating seemed no more appealing than it had in the air force. For the first time in years, his future was wide open. Chances were, a girlfriend would only influence his decisions. Even if he was a little lonely at times, life was much easier as a bachelor.

Chapter 3

G RACE ZIPPED HER raincoat up to her chest and tucked long brown strands beneath her hood. *Rain, rain, go away. Come again another ... season.* One month into spring and she'd already invented her own version of the childhood song she used to sing to Liam.

Thunder rumbled from above as she ran through the big backyard behind the bed-and-breakfast. She dashed past the fallen patio furniture, her tennis shoes sinking into the wet grass. Ignoring the water seeping into her socks, she stopped in front of the shed and unlocked the door. The wind yanked it from her grasp and pushed it wide open, creating a crack near the hinge.

She let her head roll back in frustration. *One more thing to add to her to-do list.*

The rain fell faster, and heavy drops landed on her forehead and slipped down her cheeks. She ran back for each patio chair and set them inside the shed. It was too windy to let the lightweight chairs stay outside where they could easily blow away. Hopefully, they would generate more sales by next year and they could afford to pay for nicer patio furniture.

Once all the chairs were inside the shed, she dashed into the kitchen and slipped out of her jacket and shoes.

Heavy hail pounded on the roof. The warning siren blared, its shrill noise indicating a change in the severity of the storm.

This wasn't good. The levee wouldn't be able to hold out much longer if the storm continued at this pace.

"I got a call from Knox Bennett." Mom stood at the stove and poured hot water into a teapot. "His church group will be here soon."

"I'll go into the foyer to wait for them." The church group had made reservations to stay for the week to help sandbag in nearby towns. Over the last month, the only guests they'd had were sandbagging volunteers.

A few minutes later, she pulled back the curtains in the foyer. A handful of people scrambled out of a large van, carrying duffle bags over their heads as they dashed inside.

She swung open the front door. "Welcome to Cedar Crest. I'm Grace, one of the owners."

A stylish man wearing a button-down shirt and dress pants shook her hand. "I'm Knox Bennett and these are my friends, Courtney, Zane, and Joey."

"I'm so glad you're here." She glanced out the rain-splattered window, her stomach tightening. "I'm sorry to do this to you after you just arrived, but we need to go to the basement until the storm lets up."

The guests exchanged frustrated glances but stayed quiet as they followed her along the hallway and down the steps into her basement apartment.

"Make yourselves at home." She gestured to the leather couches in her living room, then turned on the TV above the mantel and switched to the local news. "Excuse me. I'll be right back."

She strode into her bedroom and grabbed her cell phone to call Amanda. No answer. She tried again with the same results.

She walked back into the living room, forcing herself to smile. The guests didn't need to see her tension.

On TV, the weatherman pointed to a map of Orick Hills and the surrounding areas. "The thunderstorm warning will be in effect until 3:00 p.m." An image of the Mississippi River appeared next to the weatherman. "There is a flash flood warning for Maple Valley. The levee broke just minutes ago. Citizens of Maple Valley are being alerted to evacuate immediately."

The blood ran out of Grace's face. *No, no, no.* She pressed a hand against her stomach, unable to hide her concern. Where was Caleb? Where were Amanda and Ethan? Did they know the levee had broken? Were they safe?

CALEB TOSSED AND turned in bed as his subconscious flitted from one memory to the next. The soldier with his shredded hands hanging limply off the sides of a stretcher. His crew navigating the agricultural rows of the green zone as they carried a Georgian trooper with no legs. Flying in his last mission, seeing the pain from the gunshot wound reflected in Seth's features. *"Don't you dare apologize,"* Seth said. *"I'm the one who's sorry."*

His eyelids flung open. He sat up and hunched forward, resting his head in his hands. Sweat trickled down his back. He took several slow breaths to steady his heart rate. *Man, I miss you, buddy.*

Across the room, the *Fast and Furious* marathon still played on TV as it had been before he'd decided to take a nap. As sports cars raced through the streets of Los Angeles, the volume grew louder. He must've fallen asleep during the first movie.

Ignoring the racing scene, he glanced at his closet, where Seth's box of belongings sat on the top shelf. After coming home from the wake, he'd stashed the box there. His grief had been too fresh to look through the contents. But maybe if he looked through the box, he would get some sense of peace and the nightmares would go away.

He rolled out of bed and stumbled to the closet.

His cell phone vibrated on the nightstand, followed by a generic ring tone he had yet to change. Whoever was calling could wait. He'd stalled long enough. He couldn't let the box sit unopened forever.

He set it down on the floor, opened the lid, and peered inside. Seth's belongings were packed into two neat piles.

A high-pitched siren went off, its rhythmic scream blaring over the TV volume. His cell phone rang again, this time followed by a chime. Someone had left a voicemail.

The hair on the back of his neck stood on edge. Something was wrong. He quickly shoved the box back on the top shelf of his closet and picked up his cell. Both calls were from Dad.

His eyebrows pinched together as he listened to the voice mail. Dad yelled over a loud sound in the background. At first, Dad's words were overpowered by the noise, then became a little clearer before Dad unexpectedly hung up.

The phone slipped through Caleb's fingers and clattered to the floor. The few words he could understand were all he needed to hear. *The levee broke.*

The overpowering noise must've been the flood. His heart picked up speed again, racing hard and fast as he yanked jeans on over his boxers and tugged a shirt on over his bare chest. He sprinted into the living room and glanced out the window of his first-floor apartment.

The Mississippi River gushed down Ashmend Road, carrying tree branches, rocks, and fencing. People dashed out of downtown stores, their mouths open in screams, though the only sound in his apartment came from the ferocious downpour. The brick road and sidewalks were no longer visible underneath the muddy water. The force of the flood knocked over streetlamps and carried off dumpsters. Water crashed into one building after the next, breaking windows and spewing debris everywhere.

His whole body tensed. Hopefully, Dad and Amanda were on their way out of town. With the power and depth of the flood, he wouldn't be able to get to their house on the riverfront.

But he could do something. He flung open the door to his apartment, gasping as water rose up to his ankles. He dodged around the people running away from the river and ran against the current.

He dashed into each store, calling out to see if anyone was still inside. The Canine Palace, Charger's Sporting Goods, and Val's Diner were vacant. He tugged on the door to Dill's Grocery, pulling it against the water that now leveled at his calves. "Is anyone in here?"

"Yes," a boy screamed.

"Where are you?"

"Aisle twelve. I'm stuck!"

Caleb hurdled over carts and fallen shelves to the

middle of the store, his soaked shoes becoming heavier with each step. But he refused to slow down. Some of the taller shelving units had fallen over. If one of them fell on top of the boy, it could kill him.

"Where are you?" The boy's voice rose an octave higher.

"I'm almost there." Caleb turned the corner into aisle twelve.

The boy pushed at a shelf that had fallen on his legs. Cans of vegetables floated in the murky water next to him.

Poor kid. "Let me help you." He crouched down beside the boy. "Do you think your legs are broken?"

The boy shook his head.

"Good."

"Can you get me out?" The boy flicked dark blond hair away from his forehead.

"Yeah. As soon as I lift this shelf, you need to move out of the way."

"All right."

"One, two, three." He took a deep breath and lifted the shelf, then held it a few feet off the ground. His biceps trembled. As soon as the boy scooted backward, he let go. The shelf fell into the water, splashing debris onto his jeans. "Let's get out of here. I'll carry you, so we can move faster."

"No. I'm fine." The boy lifted his chin, pulled back

his shoulders, and plastered a tough-boy look on his face. But the moisture building in his eyes gave his fear away. He scrambled to a standing position and picked his feet up one at a time, ambling a few feet forward.

Caleb scrubbed a hand over his mouth. The kid didn't realize the danger they were in. "What's your name?"

Sighing, the boy stopped and turned around. "Davis."

Davis's answer gave him just enough time to move forward and pick him up.

Davis squirmed. "I said I could walk. Put me down."

"No." He clutched the kid tighter as he slowly made his way to the front of the store. Each step was harder than the last with Davis trying to wriggle free.

Finally, they made it outside. Caleb stopped for a moment, his chest puffing in and out with each labored breath. His thighs disappeared beneath the murky water that lapped against the storefronts and flowed through shattered windows. The post office mailbox floated by, inches away from smashing into them. Across the street, a Labradoodle doggy-paddled frantically with his head above the water.

Davis stopped moving and his eyes widened. "Are we gonna die?"

"Close your eyes and hold on tight." Caleb trudged through the water, letting the current push him as he headed up the steep street that led toward the edge of town. He had to get them out of here as fast as possible.

❧❀❧

GRACE TUGGED ON the freshly washed comforter to straighten out the wrinkles. She quickly positioned the throw pillows against the white wooden headboard, then strode into the attached bathroom. She hung up the bath towels, opened the white-laced curtains, and put the fuzzy white mat on the black and white tiled floor.

After her moment of panic, she'd called Amanda again. Her friend finally answered, and Grace offered to let anyone from Maple Valley stay at Cedar Crest for the night.

Amanda, Ethan, and Ray were the first guests to arrive. Then, Amanda and Ethan had taken Ray's fishing boat and gone back to search for others. Every couple of hours, more Maple Valley citizens arrived, and more were on their way.

Now that the third-floor bedrooms had fresh linens, all twelve rooms were ready. She was ready.

Scratch that, just Cedar Crest was ready.

She was not.

Grace rubbed her throbbing temples. She hadn't stopped to take a break in over three hours. Partly because she'd never had to prepare all twelve rooms at the same time and partly because Amanda hadn't found Caleb yet.

Why hadn't they found him? Where was he? For now, his safety mattered more than the awkwardness of having him stay at her bed-and-breakfast.

Outside, a car horn honked, followed by doors closing.

Knox was back. He'd made several trips in his van to meet Amanda and Ethan's boat at the edge of Maple Valley, then he drove people to Cedar Crest. But with midnight approaching, Amanda and Ethan weren't going out again. It was too dark to drive the boat.

Grace peered out the third-floor window. The porch light cascaded over the parking lot, but no one was outside. Amanda, Ethan, and Knox must have already gone in. Was Caleb with them?

She forced her feet to move out of the bedroom and down the stairs, one step at a time.

A familiar husky voice carried from the foyer.

She stopped mid-step and gripped both sides of the railing. Ribbons of warmth wrapped around her body. Caleb was safe.

Caleb was *here*.

Now that she knew he was okay, the tension disappeared from her chest and snaked down to the pit of her stomach. She turned around to go back upstairs.

The bell on the front desk dinged with a high-pitched chime.

Grace gnawed on her fingernail. *Get a grip. Be a professional.* Shaking off the nerves, she inched down the rest of the staircase until the new visitors came into view. Her gaze immediately flitted to Caleb.

He stood in the entryway with a wet shirt clinging to his well-defined chest and chiseled abs. His short blond hair lay matted against his forehead and streaks of dirt were plastered across his sun-kissed face.

Whoa. She tried to keep her jaw from falling open. Caleb was ripped and filthy. The combination was undeniably sexy. Her cheeks warmed as if everyone in the room could read her thoughts.

Amanda cleared her throat. "Thank you so much for letting us stay here tonight."

"What?" She tucked a strand of hair behind her ear and glanced at Amanda. "Oh, uh, yeah."

A boy stepped forward, jamming his hands in his pockets. "Can I stay here too?"

Grace stared at him for a moment. Where had she seen him before? He looked about the same age as Liam. "Of course, you can stay. Do you need to call your parents? Do they know you're safe?"

The boy shrugged. "I'm fine on my own. My dad's out of town for work, and I don't know where my mom is. She was working at Val's Diner when the flood hit."

She exchanged a concerned look with Amanda. "We

should call your mom. I'm sure she's worried sick about you." Before he had a chance to respond, her eyebrows rose with recognition. "You're Davis, aren't you?"

"Yeah." He crossed his arms. "How did you know?"

"You play baseball. Your team …" She let the sentence trail off. She'd almost said *beat my son's team last week*. But she was *so* not ready to talk about Liam, and Caleb had been through enough tonight.

Amanda put her hand on Davis's back and led him to the front desk. "Let's go call your mom."

Amanda's fiancé flicked thick brown hair out of his eyes. "Grace, would you mind showing us to our rooms? I can barely keep my eyes open."

Nodding, she signed them in to the guest book and reached for two sets of keys. "Follow me." Walking up to the third floor, she was acutely aware of Caleb behind her, like a static charge running through her body.

She stopped in front of an empty room and unlocked the door. She glanced at Caleb. "This is your room."

He opened his mouth, then shook his head as if he couldn't decide what to say. Instead of saying anything, he grabbed the key from her and disappeared inside his room.

She blinked. So that was how he wanted it to be. She was giving him a place to stay and he had yet to say a word to her. Ignoring her, as if she'd never mattered to him, stung more than she would've expected.

45

She quickly showed Ethan to his room, then returned to the foyer to check on Davis. "Did you get a hold of your mom?"

"She's on her way." He tucked his chin to his chest, sending wet, shaggy hair across his forehead. "But she doesn't have enough money for us to stay here."

"That's all right. You and your mom are welcome to stay for free tonight. We'll figure out the logistics tomorrow."

"I'll stay with him until his mom gets here," Amanda said.

"Thanks." In a trance-like state, Grace made her way downstairs to her apartment. She collapsed on her bed and stared up at the ceiling. How surreal that Caleb was upstairs, sleeping under the same roof. Maybe he was taking a shower right now, cleaning off all that dirt and grime. The image of his bare chest and chiseled abs brought heat pooling low in her stomach.

Her brain quickly caught up to her body, pushing away thoughts of Caleb and letting the reality of the situation sink in. Whether she was ready or not, Caleb was about to meet Liam.

Chapter 4

CALEB'S MOUTH WATERED as he sat down in the last empty chair at the dining room table. Beside him, Valerie Swanson looked up from her plate and mumbled a greeting before she continued eating.

He cut into a loaf of bread, grabbed two steaming pieces of bacon, and scooped several large spoonfuls of scrambled eggs onto the plate in front of him. He shoveled the scrambled eggs into his mouth and consumed the bacon within seconds. Each bite made him feel a little less like a wild animal and a little more human.

The only problem with being human was a full-functioning brain. A brain that would prefer to forget yesterday—the flood, the dismantled state of Maple Valley, and the fact that he was stuck at Grace's bed-and-breakfast with no other place to go.

Not that he would complain. It was kind of her to let everyone stay for free last night. He should have told her thank you, but seeing her last night resurrected long-forgotten anger that he'd buried.

He bit off a piece of warm bread. What was wrong with him? Ever since leaving the air force, he'd dealt with anger simmering just beneath the surface, sometimes boiling over without warning. Maybe he'd been this way for a while and hadn't realized it. In the air force, he'd always had an outlet—burning off steam during rescue missions. Where was he supposed to burn off steam now?

Valerie rose from the table, flattening her black shiny hair with the palms of her hands. "I'm going home to assess the damage. Want to join me?"

"Thanks for the offer, but I'm waiting for my dad to wake up. We're meeting my sister and her fiancé at my dad's house."

"Oh. Of course." She touched his forearm. "If you need anything, let me know."

"Okay." Caleb poured coffee into a mug and leaned back in his chair, admiring the modern décor of the dining room. A long chalkboard with Welcome Home written in big curly lettering hung in the middle of a gray wall. A row of off-white cabinets ran along the opposite wall, topped by a black quartz countertop that held extra plates, silverware, and condiments.

And the dining room table. *Whoa.* It was remarkable. He ran his fingers along the edge of it, admiring the marble veneer.

How impressive. If Grace had been the one to restore

and decorate this old mansion, she had a real knack for interior design.

A lanky boy with jet-black hair strode into the room, bent down in front of the row of cabinets, and pulled out a big tub of Legos. He awkwardly held the tub while shutting the cabinet door, then dropped the box. Legos scattered across the floor. "Crap. Mom's gonna kill me," he muttered.

"I can help you." Caleb moved down to the floor.

The boy's eyes grew wide. "I didn't realize breakfast was still going on. I'm not supposed to be in here until it's over. It usually closes at ten."

"It was a late night for a lot of us." Caleb hunched over, picking up Lego pieces and dropping them in the plastic tub. "Are you from Maple Valley? I don't recognize you."

"No. I live here."

"In Orick Hills?"

"Yeah, my mom owns this place."

Caleb let go of the Legos in his hand. The kid couldn't be Grace's, could he? She wasn't wearing a wedding ring. Maybe she was dating the kid's father or had gone through a divorce. Either way, it still didn't seem plausible. The kid had to be about ten. That wouldn't make sense. Unless …

The blood ran out of his face. Unless she'd had the boy when she was eighteen, after their senior year of high school.

No way. That couldn't be. Maybe she owned the bed-and-breakfast with a friend, and this kid was her friend's son. He had to make sure. "Who is your mom?"

"Grace Cunningham." The boy stopped collecting Legos and glanced at Caleb.

For the first time, he got a good look at the kid's face. The boy looked just like Grace, except for his green eyes. And yet, something about his eyes looked familiar too.

"Are you okay? You're as white as a ghost. Are you sick? My mom says I look like a ghost when I'm sick. We have a thermometer. I can go get it."

"Er, uh, no. I'm not sick. I didn't know Grace had a son."

"Yup." The boy picked up the last Lego piece and stood with the tub. "I'm Liam, by the way. Who are you?"

"C-Caleb."

"You didn't help me all that much. But it was nice to meet you." Liam walked out of the room, seemingly ready to go about his day.

His jaw tightened. Grace had moved because she was pregnant. And there was no way Liam was Caleb's son. They'd never had sex.

His hands curled into fists. She'd cheated on him, gotten pregnant, then moved before he could find out.

What a coward. She didn't even have the guts to admit her betrayal.

Without another thought, he punched his fist into a nearby cabinet. The sound of broken wood slashed through the room. He retracted his hand from the hole, marched out of the dining room, and strode outside without looking back.

He paced back and forth on the front porch. How could she have cheated on him? Especially when he'd respected her wishes to wait until they were married.

His nostrils flared. He might not have said anything to her last night, but he had plenty to say now. Which was exactly why he needed to leave for the day.

❧

LATER THAT AFTERNOON, Caleb lifted an oar out of the murky water and pushed it against the front door of his childhood home. The door didn't budge. He gripped the oar tighter and pushed harder, wincing as pain shot from his bruised hand, through his forearm, up to his bicep.

What a mistake, punching Grace's cabinet.

After taking a long walk this morning, his anger had worn off and been replaced by disappointment. Grace wasn't the person he'd thought she was. He was usually good at reading people and situations. In the air force, he had only seconds to assess the danger on the ground before deciding if he should land the aircraft to save wounded soldiers in the midst of combat. Of course, his intuition had failed him the day that Seth died.

Obviously, it had failed him with Grace too. But he and Grace had spent all of high school as a couple. How had he missed the signs indicating her true character?

Thankfully, he hadn't had much time to dwell on it. After his walk, he'd met Dad outside of Cedar Crest, and they'd headed to Maple Valley. His apartment was a wreck. Everything he just bought to furnish the place was damaged. He found his war medals, Seth's box, and the clothes he'd stored on the top shelf of his closet. After packing up the items, they paddled the boat to Dad's house.

Caleb jammed the oar against the door, and it opened just enough for the boat to pass through. He paddled the small boat inside the house and almost dropped the oar.

Picture frames, Mom's vases, and sports magazines floated through the room. A fish hopped over the top of Dad's favorite recliner. Moss lay strewn across the big screen TV that had broken away from the wall.

"Holy tarnation." Dad ran a trembling hand over the short white tufts of hair that had started to grow back after chemo. "It's worse than I imagined."

Caleb gave a slow nod. "We'll check every room and see what we can salvage."

"Yeah," Dad said, barely above a whisper.

"It's going to be okay." Caleb lowered himself out of the boat to get a better look around the house. Cold water rose up to his hips. Shivering, he moved a few feet into the living room. The flood had left its mark on every surface.

"Get me out of here." The boat wobbled back and forth as Dad rose to a standing position. "You're not doing this alone."

"I know. Amanda and Ethan should be here soon."

Dad folded his arms across his chest, the defiant gesture exposing his thin frame. "This is my home. I'm getting out of this boat whether you help me or not."

He wanted to tell Dad that it wasn't worth the risk of getting sick. But the old man wouldn't listen anyway. This was the house his parents had built together and seeing it in this dismantled state had to be devastating.

Frowning, Caleb held out his hand and helped Dad into the water.

A minute later, he waded through the hallway to assess the damage in the bedrooms. Chills ran through his body, sinking into his bones. This couldn't be his childhood home. The furniture was ruined, the mattresses were soaked and contaminated, and the clothes and shoes inside the closets were soggy and muddy.

He slowly shook his head. So far, nothing was salvageable.

"Look what I found."

Caleb followed his dad's voice into the kitchen.

Dad leaned against the countertop, clutching Mom's hand-written recipe book. He opened the worn brown cover and ran his wrinkled fingers over the yellowed pages. "It's completely dry. All three generations of recipes."

A smile tugged at his lips. "Do you remember when Mom would ask Amanda and me to help her cook? We were ready to start baking and she'd grin, point to a page, and tell us a story about grandma or great-grandma. I think she had a story to go with every recipe."

"She did." Behind thick lenses, Dad's eyes glistened.

Almost twelve years had passed, and the mention of Mom still caused Dad pain. Growing up, Caleb had hoped to have a marriage like theirs one day. They always worked as a team. As kids, if Caleb or Amanda asked to go somewhere, both of his parents had to agree. Even when Mom's depression worsened, Dad stuck by her side, attending therapy with her, and making sure she took her medications.

When she committed suicide, Dad lost it. He didn't know how to move on without her. He stayed in bed for weeks. He retired from coaching the Maple Valley football team, he stopped helping with homework, even stopped asking Caleb and Amanda if they'd turned in their college applications.

The night of the high school senior party was the first time Dad had stepped back into his role as a parent. He showed up, yelled at Amanda and Caleb and made them leave the party, then grounded them for drinking.

As mad and embarrassed as Caleb was, he'd also been relieved. His dad was back.

With every passing year, Dad moved on a little more. He opened the Canine Palace and became a business owner. And the bravery and optimism he'd shown during his recent cancer treatment was inspiring. He never complained, even though he must've been scared. He must've wondered, *Why me?*

Even now, with his house in shambles, Dad's attention was on the cookbook—the one possession that wasn't ruined.

A boat motor shut off outside, followed by a splash and quiet voices. A minute later, Amanda and Ethan waded inside the house. Amanda stared at the living room in dismay. Her cheeks glistened from already-shed tears. "Is that Mom's recipe book?"

Dad nodded. "Yeah, Minnow, it is."

Amanda trekked through the open, yet crowded, space and hugged Dad, then Caleb. She stood still with her cheek pressed against Caleb's chest.

He wrapped his arms around her. "Please tell me your new house is better off than this."

She pulled back and wiped tears off her cheeks with

her shirtsleeve. "Better, but—" She choked back a sob.

Ethan moved to stand beside her and put his arm around her shoulders. "The basement is flooded, and the main level needs new flooring in every room. There could be electrical or plumbing issues too, but we'll need to hire someone to check."

"Have you seen your apartment yet?" Amanda asked.

"We went there first. I have my war medals and a few other things, but most of my stuff is ruined."

"Oh no. I'm so sorry." Amanda sniffled. "I guess we'll all be staying at Cedar Crest for a while."

He stiffened. Once he talked to Grace, there was no way he would stay there. He'd rather sleep on a park bench.

Dad closed the recipe book and pressed it against his chest. "I won't be staying at the bed-and-breakfast any longer."

"Why not?" Amanda asked.

"Sandy offered for me to stay with her. Her house doesn't have much damage. Her injuries from the fire are still healing, and she needs an extra hand around the house."

Lucky Dad. "I'm not staying at Cedar Crest either."

Amanda pursed her lips. "I don't suppose Sandy offered for you to stay at her house too?"

"No."

"Where are you going, then?" she asked.

"I don't know yet." His anger flickered back to life, the coals of his emotions still simmering beneath the surface. "What I *do* know is that Grace cheated on me, got pregnant, and moved away without having the guts to tell me about her son." He waited to see the shock on his sister's face, but she looked oddly composed.

"That's not what happened, Caleb."

"You knew about her son and didn't tell me? How long have you known?"

"Grace told me about Liam last year. I wanted to tell you, but it's not my story to tell. You need to hear it from Grace."

He gritted his teeth and rolled his shoulders back, trying to ease the tension in his muscles. Liam was Grace's son, and she'd slept with someone else while they were dating. That part he knew for sure. What part of the story was he missing?

❧

FADING SUNLIGHT POURED through the small basement near the ceiling. Grace turned on the overhead light above the stove and pressed the spatula into the pan to break up the sizzling hamburger meat. She hummed as she tossed leftover scrambled eggs, green peppers, and diced tomatoes in the pan.

Cooking for a full house of guests was exactly what

she'd signed up for when she decided to own Cedar Crest. After speaking with the guests, most of them were planning to stay. Thankfully, insurance would cover their stay until their homes were deemed safe. It was a win-win for all of them.

For now, at least. Too bad the bed-and-breakfast couldn't stay full forever. Once the Maple Valley guests left, she would be stuck with a quiet mansion. Without guests, she was just a homeowner with way too much space.

Had she made the wrong choice to become a bed-and-breakfast owner? Loving a career wasn't enough to create a thriving business. She'd enjoyed being a social worker too, but there was something special about serving people, giving them a place to stay, and creating an atmosphere where they could relax. A home away from home.

The floor creaked as someone approached from the hallway and knocked. "I'll be right with you." She twisted the stove knob to a simmer and turned around. Caleb's large frame filled the open doorway. He stood with his legs shoulder-width apart and his hands slipped into his jean pockets. He almost looked casual, except for the hard set of his chiseled jaw. "We need to talk."

Heat flushed beneath her cheeks. *Did he know?*

"I met your son this morning."

Yup. She held her elbows tightly against her sides.

"How old is he?"

She glanced down at the floor. This was it. The moment Caleb would know why she'd ended things. "He's ten."

Caleb stepped into the kitchen; his blue eyes blazing. "Did you cheat on me?"

Her knees threatened to buckle beneath her. She moved to the prep table and pulled out a stool. "We should sit."

He sat on the opposite side of the table, crossing his arms.

She tried not to notice the way his biceps bulged beneath his sleeves and instead, met his gaze. "Do you remember the night of our senior party? How we got into that fight?"

He gave a slow nod. "I told you I wanted to sign up for the air force but that I didn't want you to change your plans to go to college."

"Well, I didn't want to have a long-distance relationship. I planned to travel with you and take online classes."

He shook his head. "I wasn't going to let you do that just because my dad spent all of my college savings on my mom's funeral. You worked hard in high school, and you deserved to have all the experiences that college had to offer."

She bit her lip, wishing she hadn't mentioned their

fight. She didn't want to rehash it. "We never finished that conversation because your dad showed up and made you leave. After you left, I was upset, so I stayed and played drinking games." She clasped her clammy hands together. "I blacked out at some point, but I vaguely recall walking home with a few people."

Caleb shifted on the stool and rested his elbows on the countertop.

"On the way, I had to throw up. Everyone else kept walking, so I thought I was alone." She took a shaky breath, then blew it out slowly. "But when I started walking again, someone grabbed me from behind."

His shoulders noticeably tensed. "Grace—"

"Let me finish." She unclasped her hands and pushed back her shoulders. It was time to tell him the truth. "I completely sobered up at that point and tried to get away. But the person was too strong and fast. He pulled me over to the playground equipment and yanked up my skirt. He held me down the whole time ... and when it was over, he ran off."

Caleb sat rigid for a moment, staring at her as the truth sunk in. He opened his mouth, then closed it. His eyes filled with compassion and sincerity, stirring something deep inside her. "I'm so sorry that happened to you."

"I'm sorry I didn't tell you sooner."

He put his hand over hers, his touch warm and firm.

"Why didn't you?"

She twisted her lips. "For the longest time, I thought it was my fault. I shouldn't have had so much to drink. I shouldn't have worn that tank top or my short skirt. I should've called my mom to pick me up from the party instead of walking home."

The skin between his brows creased together. "It's not your fault. I hate that you thought that, even for a second."

Grace gave him a half-hearted smile. "Thanks. I don't blame myself anymore." She looked down at his big hand, still covering her own. "I thought about telling you right after it happened, but I figured you'd blame me too."

Caleb tilted his head slightly, a mixture of confusion and frustration crossing his handsome features. It seemed like he was about to say something, but then he noticeably swallowed and remained silent.

She took his silence as a sign to continue. "When I told my mom I was pregnant, she suggested that I apply to other colleges, far away from Maple Valley. My mom wanted us to live someplace where no one knew us, so we could start over. Since it sounded much better than facing you and my friends, I agreed."

Caleb moved his hand and straightened his posture. "I wish you would've told me instead of running away."

Running away. The words stung. It made her sound

like a coward. Was that how he would view her now? She lifted her chin. "I did what I thought was best at the time."

"I would've been there for you." A faraway look clouded his eyes before his soft gaze hardened. "Who did it to you?" he asked in a quiet tone.

She cleared her throat. He wouldn't like her answer. "I don't know. I was grabbed from behind, and I never saw his face."

"Who walked home with you?"

"I don't remember."

He scratched behind his head. "You seem so content. Don't you want to know who did it?"

"I used to. I've replayed every second from that night, trying to figure it out, but it's not important anymore. Liam is everything to me, and I don't need to know in order to have closure."

Caleb gave a curt nod, stood, and walked around the kitchen island. "I'm glad you told me. I'm sure it wasn't easy." He put his palm on her cheek, tenderly stroking her skin with his thumb. "Good night, Grace." He walked out of the kitchen, then quickly turned around. "By the way, I'm the one who broke your cabinet in the dining room. I punched it when I thought you cheated on me."

Her eyes widened.

"I'll fix it in the morning."

She watched him walk away and slowly rose to finish breakfast preparations for the next day. His reaction had been kind and thoughtful, but did he understand why she'd made those decisions?

She stirred the egg dish and set it aside, then grabbed a ball of dough and threw it on the prep table. If it were possible, she would go back in time and tell everyone the truth right away. Maybe she would've discovered who had raped her. Maybe she and Caleb would've worked things out.

She pressed the rolling pin over the dough using short, frantic movements. She continued rolling until the dough was so thin that she had to peel it off the table and roll it back into a ball.

Hindsight is twenty-twenty. She couldn't change the past. Back then, guilt had been a dark storm cloud overpowering her mind and body. During one of her therapy sessions, her counselor had said that people experience stages of grief in different orders and for varying amounts of time.

At first, she had gone into denial. But Liam's impending arrival couldn't be ignored. After that, she'd gotten angry, mostly at herself. It was her fault, because if she could have stopped it from happening back then, then she could keep it from happening to her again.

When she'd finally come to terms with the truth— that she had no control over it—the powerlessness almost overwhelmed her. She took a year off from college and spent the majority of her days in counseling, allowing herself to heal and become whole again.

She squeezed the ball of dough so hard it oozed between her fingers. For some inexplicable reason, she wanted Caleb to understand everything she'd been through. She wanted him to understand *her*.

But she had to be realistic—she'd shut him out for eleven years. He might never understand her. She was a very different woman from the girl he'd dated in high school.

Chapter 5

MAPLE VALLEY CITIZENS filed into Rex Mathes Elementary School, their solemn conversations sounding like a quiet hum through the gymnasium.

Caleb unfolded the last row of chairs. "This doesn't seem like enough. Are there chairs anywhere else?"

Mayor Jennings pinched the bridge of his nose. "The principal only unlocked the gym storage closet for us. I can't get into any of the other closets."

"Do you want me to—" Before he could finish the question, Jennings strode toward the other side of the gym, where they'd set a podium and a microphone for tonight's city council meeting.

What was up with the mayor? Jennings had been edgy ever since they'd arrived at the elementary school to set up. It seemed unlikely that he'd be nervous. He wasn't the type of guy who got rattled easily. And the purpose of tonight's meeting was to boost the town's morale and discuss the rebuilding process. That was what he'd written on the flyer he'd emailed to everyone.

Something was bothering the mayor, but Caleb could barely focus on Jennings since his mind was still reeling from Grace's confession.

Someone had taken away her innocence. He gripped the back of a chair. Who had done it? It must've been someone they'd known. Most likely someone who attended the senior party. But all those people were their friends.

Amanda and Ethan walked inside the gym hand in hand, smiled at Caleb, and found seats toward the front. A few minutes later, Dad and Sandy arrived. Caleb waved, but the old man didn't notice as he laughed at something Sandy said.

Huh. Caleb's lips parted. Dad didn't talk much about Sandy. Had they always been good friends or were they growing closer now that Dad was staying with her?

More people filed inside the gym: Charlie, Dad's business partner; his wife, Mac; their sister-in-law, Hannah; several police officers; a few firefighters; and most of the downtown business owners.

He gave each person a long, hard look. So many people had been at the party that night, not just seniors. Many of the younger classmen had shown up, plus several college-age students who were home for the summer. One of them had been Charlie's brother, Daniel, who was now in prison for the second-degree murder of Charlie's first wife. If Daniel was the type of person to kill his sister-in-law, he could have also raped Grace.

And yet, any other guy could've done it too. It was probably impossible to know now. If Grace didn't want to pursue the truth, he needed to let it go. Eventually. It would take a while to get to that point.

If only he had taken her home when his dad made him leave, then nothing would've happened to her. It was frustrating to know his own actions could've changed the outcome.

But he had to admit, he was frustrated with Grace too. When she chose not to tell him, she'd chosen to give up on them, on him. She hadn't given him the chance to be by her side, to support her and help her heal.

The mayor tapped the microphone with his pudgy finger. "Take a seat, please."

Caleb scanned the crowded room, looking for an empty chair.

In the back row, Valerie stood and waved. She cupped her hands around her mouth, whispering loudly, "Over here."

Nodding, he strode toward Valerie and settled onto the folding chair next to her. "Thanks for saving me a seat."

"Of course." A wide smile spread across her face, showcasing her pearly white teeth.

Jennings adjusted the microphone closer to his

mouth, causing a loud screeching noise. His face turned several shades of red. "I'd like to thank you for coming tonight. For those of you who had significant damage to your homes, I'm deeply sorry." He put his hand over his chest. "We are fortunate that no one was killed, though. We are lucky in that regard."

Several people in the crowd nodded in agreement.

"There was a one in one thousand percent chance of this happening. The back-to-back thunderstorms dumped more than eight inches in just three hours, and after the final storm, a total of fifteen inches had fallen."

Jennings scanned the large room from left to right. "All of the riverfront homes need to be rebuilt. The downtown area, Hope Church, our community center, and the apartment complex need to be gutted and remodeled. Twenty-one homes need their basements or first floors remodeled."

Sniffles erupted through the gym. The atmosphere was more like a funeral than a city council meeting. Dad pulled a tissue out of Sandy's purse and gave it to her. Mac reached for Charlie's hand, squeezing it. Amanda rested her head on Ethan's shoulder.

He clasped his hands together and folded them over his knee. So many couples. So many people who could settle down and commit to doing life together. The idea of being stuck in one place with one person seemed stifling, like a claustrophobic person trapped in a small closet.

The mayor loosened the knot in his tie. "So far, we've estimated the cost of damage after flood insurance to total $18 million."

Caleb let out a low whistle. The cost of the damage was close to the economic output of some of the third-world countries he'd visited in the air force.

"In a perfect world, my hope would be to put the flood behind us and get everybody working again." Jennings tucked his chin to his chest. "Unfortunately, the flood has made a serious impact that will be hard to recover from."

Caleb furrowed his eyebrows. How was this meeting supposed to boost morale?

"We need to make a decision." Jennings blew a loud breath into the microphone. "Do we rebuild or retreat?"

The crowd erupted in conversation.

His shoulders tensed. No wonder the mayor was edgy earlier. He'd been planning to drop this bombshell on the town.

How could Jennings propose those two options? Maple Valley was their home. Amanda and Ethan planned to start a family here. Dad and Charlie had the Canine Palace, the place that had given both men a new purpose in life. It was a town where people took care of each other. Last year, the community committee had raised funds to pay for Dad's cancer treatment.

This town wasn't a dot on a map. It was a community. If they retreated, their community would be torn apart. Caleb stood, his chair skidding across the gymnasium floor. "We can't retreat. This is our home. We can come out of this stronger."

"I wish that were true, but we have to look at the numbers." Jennings ran a hand over his gray beard. "Together and individually, we'll be in debt for decades."

Sandy dabbed at her eyes. "As much as I love this town, I'm close to retirement. I can't afford to rebuild Candy Galore and start my business again."

Several store owners nodded in agreement.

Charlie stood in the front row and put his hands on his hips. "We have to find a way to raise the money and rebuild."

"Please hold your opinions." Jennings clutched both sides of the podium. "We'll take a vote at the next meeting: retreat or rebuild."

Caleb crossed his arms. He didn't blame the mayor for thinking about finances, but he would not let Maple Valley be torn apart for good.

※

GRACE STARED AT Amanda. Her lips parted in awe. "You look beautiful."

Amanda stepped up onto the carpeted platform. She

looked at her reflection in the large mirror and ran her hands along the lace fabric hugging her flat torso. "You said that about the last three dresses."

"She said it because it's true." Kendall reached for a long lace veil and handed it to Amanda. "You've looked amazing in every dress so far."

"Thanks," Amanda said in a quiet tone. She stared at the door as a large group of women entered the bridal shop.

"What's wrong?" Grace asked.

Blinking, Amanda sank to the platform in one fluid motion. She looked like a white witch melting to the ground as the skirt of the dress ballooned around her waist. "It's not supposed to be this way."

Grace rushed to Amanda's side. "What are you talking about?"

"Our church is damaged from the flood. And I wanted to have our reception in the community center." Amanda's voice hitched. "But I can't. Those buildings might not be repaired in time. Maybe they never will be. I still can't believe Maple Valley might be gone."

Grace tucked a curly strand of hair behind Amanda's ear. "Let's focus on the positive. You've found the man you want to marry for the rest of your life, and he makes you happier than I've ever seen you."

The bride-to-be bit back a smile. "That's true."

"In two short months, you'll be Mrs. Contos." Kendall sat down beside them, a wistful expression crossing her face. "You'll finally live together. You'll wake up to him every day. You'll laugh at the silly habits you have that your spouse finds weird." She took a short breath before she continued. "You'll cook together. You'll host parties together. You'll fight."

Grace scrunched her nose. "How does fighting fit in that list?"

"Well, maybe not the fight itself, but the *making up* part ..." Kendall blushed as she let the sentence trail off.

"I can't wait." Amanda laughed. "For all of it."

"Oh brother." Grace shook her head.

Kendall raised her eyebrows. "What?"

"You're romanticizing what it's like to be a newly-wed. I'm sure it *is* mostly great, but it's probably hard too. I don't think anyone should go into marriage with unrealistic expectations." She stood and took the veil from Amanda, fastening it in her friend's hair. "Then again, what do I know? I don't even remember the last time I had a date."

Amanda lifted the bottom of the veil and adjusted it around her shoulders. "Grace Cunningham, please tell me you're joking."

Her cheeks flushed. She shouldn't have brought up dating to these two. "Stop looking at me. We should focus on you today."

"Nice try." A spark of excitement flashed in Amanda's eyes. "There must be a reason you haven't dated anyone recently. Spill."

Yup, she definitely should've kept her mouth shut. "I don't have time." Raising Liam and running a new business were hard enough to balance by themselves, and now she had maid of honor responsibilities, like planning the bachelorette party and bridal shower. No way could she possibly add dating to that mix.

"What if the right guy comes along?" Amanda asked. "Someone who still cares about you?"

Her heart picked up speed. Did Caleb still have feelings for her? Even if he did, did it matter? She had loved Caleb, as strongly as any teenage girl could love a boy. But she didn't love him anymore. Her life was full and complete. Raising Liam and being a good mom were her main priorities now.

She had to make sure Amanda and Kendall wouldn't try to play matchmaker. "Your brother and I have moved on. There's nothing between us anymore."

"That's what I thought, but the way he looked at you that first night at Cedar Crest … I can tell he still has feelings for you."

A slow smile spread across Kendall's face. "Valerie's been trying to get his attention ever since he moved back, and he barely notices her. Maybe he *is* still hung up on you."

"I know the two of you want to be right, but I don't

think you are. And just so you know, I'm fine being single. I'm happy. I'm—"

One of the boutique consultants walked by, her eyes widening. "What's wrong, Amanda? Why are you sitting in that pretty dress? Do you hate it? Is it the veil? Whatever it is, I'm here to help."

"It's not the dress or the veil. I'll be ready to try the next dress on soon."

Grace pulled Amanda to a standing position. "No, you're ready now. Go."

As soon as Amanda disappeared behind the curtain, she settled back onto a chair beside Kendall. She pulled her hair over to one shoulder and braided the loose brown strands. Her silly racing heart needed to slow down. Amanda was wrong. She'd probably misinterpreted his look. Caleb had given no indication otherwise.

Amanda waltzed out of the dressing room, wearing an A-line dress with a princess scoop neckline and silk skirt.

Grace and Kendall rose from their chairs, both speaking at once. "It's b—"

"Before you say anything about the dress, I just had an idea I want to run by you." Amanda stood on the edge of the platform, moving her hands as she spoke. "If you hate it, promise me you'll be honest."

"What is it?" Grace asked.

"Could we have my wedding and reception at your

bed-and-breakfast? You have that big backyard with plenty of room for all our guests." She paused for a moment as if a new thought came to mind. "Of course, I'll have to ask our priest if he'll ordain an outdoor wedding. But I'm guessing with the damage done to our church, he'll make an exception." She blew out a breath before she continued. "Anyways, I'll help with everything, and I'll pay to rent the space."

Host the wedding and reception at Cedar Crest? It would take a lot of work to plan and prepare the backyard for such a big event, while also accommodating a full house of guests.

But how could she say no? With only two months until "I do," it would be hard for Amanda and Ethan to find new venues. They didn't need one more hiccup in their plans. "Of course."

Amanda lifted the skirt of her dress and carefully stepped off the platform, breaking the space between them. She threw her arms around Grace, wrapping her in a hug. "Thank you so much. You're the best."

Grace laughed. "By the way, I think you've found the one."

"Jeez, I hope so. I already told him yes."

"No. I'm talking about the dress." She stepped out of their embrace and eyed Amanda up and down. The sleek white fabric accented her hourglass figure in all the right places. "Take a look."

Amanda twirled in a slow circle and stared at her reflection in the mirror. Moisture built in her eyes. She waved her hand like a fan in front of her face. "It's perfect. I love it."

"I'm so happy for you." She meant it wholeheartedly, but she had to force herself to smile. Her stomach twisted in knots. She had to plan the bachelorette party and bridal shower, run Cedar Crest, and prepare for Amanda's wedding, not to mention keeping up with Liam and his schoolwork. How would she pull it off? The better question was, how would she do any of it well?

CALEB GRITTED HIS teeth and marched inside the bed-and-breakfast. It took everything in his willpower not to slam the door. The arsonist had broken into Fern's Floral, set a firework in the storage closet, and lit it.

It had taken over an hour for the firemen to travel to Maple Valley by boat and assemble their limited equipment. By the time they extinguished the fire, hours later, the building was no longer standing. It was small chunks of wood and debris floating in the river.

Caleb stepped into the living room and headed toward the stairs. A long shower and a sleeping pill would be the only way he'd sleep tonight. The arsonist who had started the fire at Candy Galore was no doubt the same person who started the fire at Fern's Floral.

Who was the culprit? What did they have against those stores? With no clues left behind, it was impossible to know. Hopefully, they'd catch the criminal soon.

"How come you're out so late?"

Caleb turned, spotting Liam on the rug. "My shift just ended. I'm a firefighter."

The boy sat hunched over a flat square Lego board with three tall buildings rising from it. He scrunched up his nose, looking just like Grace as he did it. "Wow. Did you put out any fires today?"

"Uh-huh."

"Do you ever get scared?"

"That's a good question. Can I tell you a secret?"

Liam nodded.

Caleb squatted beside the boy and spoke quietly. "I get scared all the time."

"You do?"

"Yeah."

Liam arched an eyebrow, his green eyes filled with disbelief. "How can you be a fireman, then?"

Caleb plopped down on the rug and extended his legs. "I'll tell you something I learned in the air force. It's all right to be scared. It means you're about to do something very brave."

Liam looked at Caleb in awe.

Pride radiated through his core. This must be what it felt like to be a dad, sharing life lessons with your kid. "What are you building?"

"A town." Liam pointed to three buildings. "This is the grocery store, over here is the restaurant, and this one is a school. I'm trying to figure out what I want to build next."

"What about a toy store or a pet store?"

"A pet store is a good idea. I have a dog and a cat somewhere in this box."

"I'll search for them while you start making the building."

"Okay." Liam reached for several yellow block pieces, then stuck them in a rectangular shape on the Lego board.

"Liam, it's time for—" Grace stopped behind the couch, glancing from her son to Caleb. She twisted her full, rosy lips. "Oh. Hi."

Liam looked at his mom. "Guess what? Caleb just put out a fire."

"Where?" she asked.

"Fern's Floral."

"Oh no. Poor Fern. She made the prettiest floral arrangements."

He nodded. "Unfortunately, we couldn't get there fast enough. It was in bad shape by the time we arrived."

Grace had a faraway look in her eyes as she put a

hand over her wrist. "Remember the corsage you got me for prom? It had little crystals in it and the most beautiful lavender spray roses I've ever seen."

His eyebrows furrowed together. She sounded oddly sentimental for someone who left town and never returned to see him or anybody else. Why hadn't she come back? The question was on the tip of his tongue, but now was not the time.

"Do know how the fire started?" she asked.

"An arsonist. Someone started a fire at Candy Galore too. We haven't been able to find the culprit yet."

"That's terrible. I hope you find them soon."

"Me too."

Grace glanced at her watch. "Liam, it's time for bed. You can finish your Lego town tomorrow."

Growling, Liam tilted his head back. "But Mom, that's not fair. Caleb just started building it with me. We're making a pet store."

"Instead of getting upset, could you think of a different alternative? You could ask Caleb if he wants to play with Legos again sometime."

Liam glared at Grace and crossed his arms. "We aren't *playing*. We're building." He let out a *humph* before looking at Caleb. "Will you?"

"Sure." Caleb resisted the urge to chuckle. He hadn't spent much time around a ten-year-old before. If only his own problems were as easy as finding time to build a town of Legos. "How about after breakfast tomorrow?"

Liam frowned. "I have to go to school."

"How about after dinner?"

"Okay." Liam untangled his gangly limbs and dashed out of the room, toward the basement.

Grace expelled a breath. "This new attitude has come out of nowhere. It's driving me nuts."

"I don't think you need to worry." He stood. "Liam seems like a great kid."

"He is. He's had his moments lately, but he's so passionate about everything he does. I know he'll be good at whatever he sets his mind to." She shifted her weight from one foot to the other. "This is a little off-topic, but I've been meaning to ask you, how are you doing now that you've had more time to process Seth's death?"

"I'm doing all right." Caleb scratched the back his head. "I miss him a lot."

She gave him a sad smile. "What was inside the box his mom gave to you?"

"I don't know. I started looking through it the day of the flood, but obviously, I got sidetracked."

"Have you opened it since or did it get ruined?" she asked.

"It's fine. It was at the top of my closet. I haven't opened it again, though."

"Why not?"

He shrugged. "Just waiting for the right time, I guess."

"I see." She bit her bottom lip. "It might be painful to look through his things, but you might also enjoy it."

"I doubt it," he said in a quiet tone.

"Hear me out. You were friends for a long time. You shared so many memories. It could be nice to remember."

Caleb frowned. "What's hard for me is that I feel like I failed Seth. I was the pilot the night he got shot. I should've made different choices during that mission. If I had, he might still be alive."

"Don't do that." She shook her head. "You'll drive yourself crazy."

His throat thickened with emotion. "I know, but it's hard not to think about it."

"Think about other things." Grace leaned against the back of the couch. "Do you remember when Seth moved in next door to me, and his parents put a pool in their backyard? You and Amanda came over, and we baked brownies for the Seymours. Then, we knocked on their door and introduced ourselves, secretly hoping they'd invite us to go swimming."

A smile tugged at his lips. "It worked too."

"Oh yeah. We spent the whole summer in Seth's pool."

"That was a great summer. By the end of it, I finally

got the courage to ask you on our first date."

"Oh please." Grace folded her arms across her chest. "As if *you* were scared."

"I was. I even practiced on Seth." He chuckled. "I was so bad that Seth told me I should forget it. He said I'd make a fool of myself, and I'd probably lose you as a friend."

Her eyebrows rose. "Good thing you didn't listen to him, huh?"

"I didn't take Seth seriously when it came to girls. Remember when he asked Sheila to prom by putting an ad in the school newspaper?" Caleb waited for her to nod before he continued. "I sat next to Sheila in the lunchroom when she read it. Her face turned as red as a tomato before she threw the paper at him and walked out."

"Did he date anyone while you were overseas?"

"Not really. Trust me when I say this, the guy had no game." Caleb scrubbed a hand over his face. "Thanks for asking about Seth. I'm glad I can talk about him with you."

Grace smiled. "Anytime."

He took a few steps toward the stairs. "I should get to bed. I'm beat."

A thoughtful expression crossed her face as he walked past her. "Can I ask you something?"

"Anything."

"I went dress shopping with Amanda yesterday and

she mentioned … Never mind. Forget I said anything. You're tired, and I shouldn't have brought it up."

A smirk quivered at the corners of his mouth. "I can't forget it now. Just ask."

Grace gave a flustered laugh. "Amanda thinks you still have feelings for me. I'm hoping it's not true. I would feel horrible if it was."

He tugged on his earlobe, struck by her straightforwardness. In high school, she'd always been shy while talking about her feelings. "I was shocked when you moved away, and yeah, it sucked, but to say I never got over you probably isn't accurate." He met her expectant gaze. "Things just didn't work out between us."

"That's true," she said slowly. "I'm glad we feel the same way."

He studied her face as a flicker of sadness flashed across her big brown eyes. Had he hurt her feelings? He'd meant to put her at ease.

And he'd told her the truth. But seeing her again *had* brought back unexpected feelings and forgotten memories. Like walking hand-in-hand down high school hallways. Spending their free class periods at his house, kissing until they had to go back to school. Laying on a blanket beneath the stars, talking about their future.

Why mention that to her, though? Grace deserved to date a man who was ready to settle down with her and Liam. Not someone like him, who wasn't looking for a serious commitment.

Chapter 6

L IAM TOSSED HIS sports bag in the middle of the backyard. He grabbed his baseball and mitt, then tossed the ball toward the sky. A few seconds later, it landed in the center of his mitt with a satisfying *thump*. Finally, a warm sunny day to practice.

Davis stepped outside, letting the backdoor slam behind him. He strode across the yard and stuck a piece of gum in his mouth. "Can I play?"

Liam tossed the ball from his hand to his mitt. Why would Davis want to play with *him*?

After the flood, Davis and many of the other Maple Valley kids had transferred to schools in Orick Hills. Davis had only been at Rex Mathes Elementary for three weeks, and already he was one of the most popular kids in class. And he'd never spoken to Liam once. Not at the bed-and-breakfast, at recess, or in class.

Davis put his hands on his hips, standing eye to eye with Liam. "Well?"

"Uh, sure."

"Do you have an extra mitt? Mine got ruined in the flood. My dad said he'd get me a new one, but I don't see him till next weekend."

Liam scrunched his nose. "How come?"

Davis rolled up his sleeves in jerky movements. "My parents just got divorced." He spit the wad of gum into the grass. "How come your dad's not around? Are your parents divorced too?" His tone sounded hopeful.

"No. My dad's never been around."

"He bailed on you and your mom?"

"Something like that." To end the conversation, Liam bent over his duffle bag, searching for the extra mitt. Davis didn't need to know that Mom had no clue who his dad was. During a family tree unit this year, he told his classmates, and they'd laughed at him. Mrs. Beardsley told them to stop and explained that families are made up of many different people.

His classmates had waited until recess before they started calling his mom dirty names. For most of the school year, they continued, calling her names that he had to look up on his computer.

Defending her would have only made it worse. He could ask her about his dad again, but she'd always said she would tell him more when he was older.

"Here." He tossed the mitt to Davis and jogged to the other side of the yard. He gripped the ball in his hand, trying to calm his nerves. Davis was the best pitcher in the league. Most of the guys on his baseball team had struck out during their last game against Maple Valley.

"What's wrong with you?" Davis asked.

Shrugging, he looked down at the ground. "Nothing."

"I can see you shaking from over here." Davis jogged across the yard, standing so close Liam could smell the lingering scent of bubble gum on Davis's breath. "We're on the same team now. Practicing with me can only help you."

Liam kicked at the ground before meeting his gaze. "What do you mean we're on the same team?"

"You didn't know? Maple Valley's baseball field is gone, so my team's joining your team."

Liam did a quick calculation. "That's way too many players."

"Some of my teammates aren't playing for the rest of the season. Your team had the bare minimum, so it evens out."

"Oh." At least Liam wouldn't have to play against Davis anymore, and they had a real shot of winning.

Davis ran back to his spot in the yard. "Are we gonna do this, or what?"

Liam swallowed hard. He rolled his shoulders, wound up, and threw the ball.

Davis caught it with ease and threw it back.

He could hear it coming before he saw it fly past him and land on the grass. His shoulders sagged as he waited for Davis to laugh at him, but the only sounds came from the birds chirping.

Huh. Biting back a smile, he threw the ball again. Maybe Davis wasn't such a bad guy after all.

❧

CALEB SHIFTED ON the folding chair and crossed his arms, waiting for the city council meeting to start. Even though many people said they supported rebuilding, if the mayor didn't have a solid plan, people could change their minds.

"Good evening, everyone." Jennings gripped both sides of the podium. "At our last meeting, some of you shared opinions about wanting to rebuild. I asked several developers to visit Maple Valley to determine their interest in the project. I'm happy to announce we have three offers. I haven't made an official decision yet, but we had one offer that exceeded our financial needs. I'd like you to meet the man who made the offer."

Heads turned as a familiar-looking man wearing a navy suit and baby blue tie approached the podium. With gelled hair and pearly white teeth, the guy looked like a model straight out of *GQ* magazine. "Thank you for inviting me to your meeting. I'm Knox Bennett with

Mt. Point Development."

Amanda nudged Caleb. "That's the guy who was staying at Cedar Crest when we first got there. The one who drove people back to the bed-and-breakfast after the flood."

"Oh yeah, that's right. I didn't know he was a developer, did you?"

Frowning, Amanda shook her head. "He was staying there with his church group. Have you seen him at Cedar Crest lately?"

"No, I think he left after the flood."

Behind them, Sandy let out a loud *shh*.

Caleb exchanged a look of amusement with his sister and turned his attention back to the developer.

"I'd like to extend my deepest condolences for the condition of your town. When I was a boy, my hometown was destroyed by a tornado. The entire town had to be rebuilt. Twenty years later, it's thriving better than ever before. That's what I want for Maple Valley."

Amanda raised her hand. "What are you proposing, exactly?"

Knox squared his shoulders. "Mt. Point Development would like to buy Maple Valley, erase your debt, and rebuild your town."

People shot fists in the air, shouting affirmative responses.

Caleb sat up straighter, unwilling to celebrate until

he heard all the facts. "What are your plans for rebuild-ing?" he asked loudly.

"In addition to some of your mom-and-pop shops, my company can bring in new stores, such as Walmart, Lowe's, Best Buy, Bass Pro Shops, and many others. These stores will be major additions to your local economy. You'll have more shopping options, significant growth in retail sales, more job opportunities, and added tax revenue." Knox smiled. "We're also considering adding riverfront apartments, a B&B, or a hotel."

Several conversations started at once.

Jennings waddled back to the podium and stood beside the developer. His flushed cheeks grew crimson. "One person at a time, please."

Caleb raised his hand. Adding big name stores did not sound like a good idea.

Sighing, Jennings pointed at Caleb. "Go ahead."

He stood and planted his feet in a wide stance. "Let me get this straight, Mr. Bennett. You want to buy us out, bring *some* of our local businesses back, and add *chain* stores?"

Before the developer could respond, Dad rose from his chair. "What happens to the owners and employees of the stores that aren't"—he paused to use air quotes—"brought back?"

"We'll try to keep as many of the local stores as pos-sible." Knox's tone stayed confident and unnervingly compassionate. "I understand that they're the heart of your town. The owners and employees of stores that aren't rebuilt will be the first people hired in the new stores."

Caleb folded his arms across his chest. "Maple Valley isn't just a town. It's a community; it reflects a local culture. Our stores are humanly scaled and pedestrian oriented. If you add chain stores, you're taking all of that away."

"I don't want to do that." Knox held his hands up in surrender. "My goal would be to rebuild the culture of your downtown district while giving you opportunities for new and improved growth."

"How will local businesses compete?" Dad asked. "If we don't match some of the chain's lower prices, we'll lose money on every sale. It's only a matter of time before we're forced to close."

Some of the people who had originally looked excited, now frowned.

Behind the podium, Jennings switched places with Knox and cleared his throat. "All of the developers who made offers want to add chain stores. They need a foolproof way to make their money back. Otherwise, it's a huge risk to buy flooded land and hope our little economy can overcome."

Caleb squeezed the back of his neck. What the mayor said made sense, but Maple Valley would never be the same.

"We have two big decisions ahead of us," Jennings said. "First, we need a majority vote to rebuild and hire Mt. Point Development. The second decision will be based on each individual owner at a later date. You'll need to decide if you're willing to sell your property. Any questions about that?"

The room fell silent.

"Great." The mayor lifted his hand. "All in favor of rebuilding and using Mt. Point Development, please raise your right hand."

Caleb sucked in a breath. Even if Maple Valley wouldn't be the same, at least it would still exist. It was the only option they had. He slowly raised his hand.

A few minutes passed as Jennings scanned the crowd, quietly counting. Finally, a wide smile spread across his face. He glanced at Knox. "You're hired, Mr. Bennett."

Caleb grimaced. "I hope that developer is telling the truth."

"Me too. I'm still not sure if he is, but he seemed like a nice guy when I talked to him on the night of the flood." Amanda glanced at her watch. "I have to run a few errands before I go back to the bed-and-breakfast. Would you mind getting a ride from someone else?"

"Sure. I'll see you later." He walked out of the gym, maneuvering past groups of people who had stopped to chat. He wasn't in the mood for small talk.

"Wait." A firm hand gripped his shoulder.

He turned around.

Jennings adjusted the knot of his tie, loosening it slightly. "I know you're not happy with me right now, but I'd like your help."

"With what?"

"Knox wants me to form a committee to help with the remodeling process. I think you'd be a good asset. People respect you. If you're helping with the remodel, they might be more willing to sell their properties and make the necessary changes."

"But what if I don't agree with the changes the developer wants to make?"

"That's exactly why you should be on the committee. You can voice your concerns each step of the way."

"And you'd be willing to listen?"

"We have a lot of decisions ahead of us, and I don't want to be the only one making them." Jennings patted Caleb's arm. "Trust me when I say that I want what's best for this town."

Developers only had one goal in mind—to make money. The committee was probably just a ploy, a way for Mr. Bennett to appear like a team player. But just in case the developer *was* telling the truth, Caleb had to take a chance. "All right. I'll do it."

"Thank you." Jennings smiled as he walked away.

Caleb scratched the back of his head. What had he

just gotten himself into?

❧❦❧

"HEY. I NEED a favor."

Grace balanced her cell phone between her ear and shoulder as she folded the last set of freshly washed linens. "What is it?"

Amanda blew a breath into the receiver. "Could you do my cake tasting at two o'clock this afternoon? One of my patients called. Her water just broke. I'm driving to the birth center right now."

Grace glanced at her watch. That only left an hour to finish making all the beds, but the desperation in Amanda's voice carried through the receiver and pinched her heart. Wedding planning should be one of the happiest times of Amanda's life, but nothing was going as planned for her friend. "I'd be happy to go, but are you sure you don't want to reschedule?"

"I'd like to, but Confectionary Corner was complete-ly booked when I made this appointment. I'm scared we wouldn't get in any time soon." Her voice trembled. "I'm sorry to do this to you. I know how busy you are. I tried asking Kendall first, but she can't go. Jeffrey has a double ear infection."

"That's okay." Hopefully, Mom was done with the preparations for dinner and could finish the afternoon to-do list on her own.

"Thank you so much. Ethan will meet you there. Normally, I'd be fine with him making the decision on his own, but he has some eclectic tastes. I'm scared he'll request black licorice cupcakes."

She laughed. "Are those popular in Greece?"

"No. I'm pretty sure it's just an Ethan-thing." Amanda's mood seemed significantly livelier than just a few minutes ago. "He's at our house with the construction crew, but he should be able to leave soon."

"Sounds good."

An hour later, Grace arrived at Confectionary Corner. She inhaled the sweet scents of sugar, flour, and chocolate drifting through the bakery. The long, rectangular space held about twenty tables, most of them occupied. Conversations floated through the room, sounding like a pleasant hum.

She smiled and scanned the bakery to see if Ethan was among the sitting customers. He wasn't. This would be fun, trying cake flavors with him. When she'd worked at the hospital, she'd often teamed up with Ethan's oncology department, ensuring cancer patients had both physical and emotional support throughout their treatments. Even though some days were hard, Ethan still knew how to have a good time, always making people laugh with stories about his big Greek family.

A small line had formed near the front counter, but

Ethan wasn't in line either. She eyed a broad-shouldered man looking at the display case. He wore a black sports jacket and jeans. The sun shined through the front window, highlighting the light tones of blond in his hair. Beneath one arm, he held a worn leather-bound book.

As if he sensed someone watching him, the man turned around. It was Caleb. His eyebrows rose. "Hey. What are you doing here? I thought I was meeting Amanda."

A blush rose in her cheeks for getting caught staring when she hadn't realized it was him. He cleaned up well. "One of her patients went into labor, so she asked me if I could come. Where's Ethan?"

"Their construction crew found mold in the second-floor walls. Ethan needed to stay to find out if it's in all the walls. If that's the case, he'll need to make a decision about what to do." Caleb rocked back on his heels. "He asked me if I could come instead."

"Oh." She adjusted the purse strap over her shoulder.

Caleb turned toward the front counter and addressed the red-haired woman behind the register. "We're here for the wedding cake tasting."

"Delightful." The woman wiped her palms on her flowered apron, then extended her hand to each of them. "I'm the owner, Patty Smith. I'm the one you spoke to on the phone."

Grace opened her mouth to correct Patty, but the

woman bent down and disappeared behind the counter for a moment. When she straightened, she held a bottle of champagne and two glasses. "Come with me."

As they followed her, Caleb leaned in close to Grace and whispered, "Let's enjoy this as the bride and groom."

Huh? Why would they pretend to be Amanda and Ethan? It didn't sound like a good idea.

Mainly because she'd imagined her and Caleb as a bride and groom too many times to count. In high school, she'd daydreamed about their wedding, planning the theme, colors, and centerpieces. The two of them would have stood in front of a small church while the guests cheered when the pastor announced them as Mr. and Mrs. Meyers. Then, Caleb would've swept her off her feet and kissed her in front of all their friends and family.

She pushed the thought to the back of her mind, but her stomach fluttered at the image anyway.

Caleb slid into an empty booth. Smirking, he patted the spot next to him. "I promise I won't bite, sugar-lips."

She rolled her eyes and took a seat. He filled up more than half the booth, and his arm brushed against hers. His touch sent electricity humming through her veins. She quickly set her hands in her lap.

Patty poured champagne into their glasses. "This is a complimentary bottle for your tasting today."

"Thank you." Grace took a long sip. Hopefully, the

champagne would settle her nerves.

"When we spoke over the phone, you requested a variety of cupcakes." Patty reached for two menus that were already on the table. "We have all the generic flavors, plus several unique options." She pointed to a list on the left side of the menu. "Our most popular flavors are Pink Champagne, Luscious Lemon, Key Lime, Peanut Butter Cup, Bananas Foster, and Chocolate Dream."

"They sound delicious. We'd like to sample all of those." Caleb set the leather-bound book on the table and opened it to a bookmarked page. "Could you also use this recipe for one of the cupcake flavors? It's my mom's recipe."

"Red Velvet." Patty ran her pink fingernail down the list of ingredients. "Of course. I'd be delighted. I hope I can bake it to your mom's standards."

He shifted in the booth. "My mom passed away years ago. I'd like to think a part of her will be at my wedding."

Her chest swelled. She'd forgotten how sentimental he could be.

Patty smiled. "I'll be right back with samples."

After Patty left the table, Grace turned toward Caleb. "Why are we pretending to be the bride and groom?"

"They couldn't make it. I probably won't do this again, so why not enjoy it?"

She paused for a moment. His statement brimmed with meaning. "You never want to get married?"

"I'm not sure, but I'm starting to lean toward no." He took a drink and peered at her above the rim of his glass.

"Why not?"

"I came home to spend time with my dad, but the longer I'm here, the more I wonder if I'm cut out for civilian life. Working as a firefighter is something to do, and it keeps me busy. It's not something I want to do for the rest of my life. I miss the rush and sense of purpose I used to have."

"Maybe you have a different purpose now, one you haven't discovered yet."

He gave her a knowing look. "You haven't changed. Still trying to figure it all out for everyone."

She stiffened. "What are you talking about?"

He rested his arm above the booth and faced her directly. "Like when you threw away your college acceptance letters without telling me."

"First of all, I thought you'd be happy if I came with you to basic training." She glared at him. "Secondly, are we really having this argument again?"

"I'm not trying to argue; I'm making an observation. You're a lot different from how I remember. I guess I'm happy to see parts of you I recognize. As frustrating as your planning was sometimes, the way you've always been willing to sacrifice for others is also kinda sexy."

The butterflies in her stomach returned. *Did he just call her sexy?* She finished her champagne as Patty waltzed back to the table with a binder and a platter of samples.

"I forgot to ask you over the phone if you wanted a groom's cake," Patty said. "If you do, then you'll need to pick a theme and flavor for that too."

"What's a groom's cake?" Caleb asked.

"It's influenced by the groom and represents your tastes and hobbies. It can have a theme, like Star Wars, Harry Potter, a beer keg, a sports team, or a tuxedo. Do any of those sound like you?"

His shoulders tensed.

Sensing his hesitation, Grace put her hand on his forearm. "I have an idea. Since you proposed to me at sea, what if we had a cake with a bride and groom on a boat?"

"Oh, yeah. That's a good idea," Caleb said.

Patty scribbled a note in Amanda and Ethan's file. "How romantic."

"These look delicious." Caleb rubbed his hands together. "Which one should we try first, honey?"

Honey? He was really getting into his role. Since she couldn't call him out in front of Patty, she kicked him under the table.

"Ouch."

Served him right.

Patty looked from Caleb to Grace. "I'll give you some time to yourselves to try all the samples."

"Thanks." Grace picked up a piece of Chocolate Dream and bit into it. The deliciously moist cake and sweet frosting almost melted in her mouth. She licked her lips. "Mmm, this is so good. I can see why Amanda, I mean, why many people gave this place such high praise."

Caleb leaned over with his mouth so close to her ear that a tingle shot down her spine. "Patty wasn't that far away," he whispered. "She could've heard you. You almost blew our cover."

"A cover we don't need to have." She grimaced, but she couldn't deny it was a little exhilarating, pretending to be the bride. "I can't believe you might never get married."

He picked up a piece of Bananas Foster and let it dangle on his fork. "Why is that so hard for you to believe?"

"Whenever we talked about getting married in high school, you seemed like you wanted to."

He looked at her for a moment as if he couldn't decide how to respond. Finally, he shrugged. "Things change." He bit into the cupcake, seemingly preoccupied with judging the taste. "How about you? How come you never got married?"

"It's hard to date as a single parent. I'm not just

looking for a husband, I'm looking for someone who would be a good dad. And specifically, a dad who would be good for Liam."

"When's the last time you went on a date?"

"It was too long ago to remember."

He put down his fork. "How are you going to find the right guy if you won't give anyone a chance?"

She sighed. "It's complicated. What if I have to date twenty different guys to find a husband? How would I explain that to a ten-year-old?"

"It depends, are you talking about dating them all at once?" Caleb chuckled. "You're thinking about it all wrong. You make dating seem like too much work."

"And you make it sound too simple."

He rested his elbows on the table. "What are you so afraid of?"

Was she really that transparent, or did he understand her better than most people? Either way, he was right about her being afraid. But weren't her fears justified? She couldn't think solely about herself. She was a mother. And what if she fell for someone who ended up breaking her heart? It had taken her years to get over Caleb. She couldn't put herself through that kind of heartbreak again.

"You know what you need?" Caleb wiped his mouth with a napkin and continued before she had a chance to answer. "You need to go out on a date and see how fun it can be. What do you say?"

Her heart picked up speed. "Are you asking me on a date?"

"Just think of it as an old friend helping you out. No strings attached." He winked. "And an afternoon of promised fun."

"I don't …" She stopped midsentence as red blotches appeared on his neck and traveled up to his face. "Are you okay?"

He spit into the napkin and coughed.

"What's wrong?" Her eyes widened.

Patty rushed to the table. Her face grew pale. "Are you having an allergic reaction?"

He coughed again. "Were there nuts in the Bananas Foster?"

"Yes." Patty looked at Grace. "When I spoke to you on the phone, you told me that neither of you had food allergies."

"Um, I forgot." She placed a clammy hand on his knee. They should've told Patty the truth. "How bad is your allergy? Do you need to go to the hospital?"

"No. Will you get my EpiPen from my truck, though?" He handed her the keys.

She rushed outside and found his EpiPen container in the back seat. She unzipped the bag as she ran back inside the shop. Everyone had stopped talking, their eyes focused on Caleb.

She followed their gazes and stopped mid-step, almost dropping the bag.

His jeans lay in a lump around his shoes. He stood beside their booth in his sports jacket and tight boxers that wrapped snugly around his waist and thighs.

She swallowed hard and forced herself to look up. The blotches covered his entire neck. Gaining her composure, she broke the distance between them and handed him the pen.

He quickly removed the cap with his teeth and inserted the needle in his thigh. After a few minutes, the blotches began to fade. He pulled up his jeans and gave her a sheepish grin. "Well, that was exciting, huh?"

She shook her head, pretending to disagree, but yes, it had been exciting. Just not solely in the way he meant. Heat flowed through her, thawing those areas long frozen over and sending desire coursing through her veins.

Whoa. If she didn't get control of herself, she was in big, big trouble.

Chapter 7

GRACE PUMPED HER arms and jogged faster, trying to keep up with Amanda's brisk pace. "I want to send the bridal shower invites by the end of May. Do you have a date in mind yet?"

"Let's do it the weekend before the wedding. Ethan's parents and sisters are flying in a week early and I'd like to include them."

"Are his parents happy you're having a Greek Orthodox wedding?"

"Happy is an understatement." A wide smile spread across Amanda's face. "When Ethan called to tell them that I wanted to take Greek classes, I could hear his mom crying. Then, she started rambling in Greek. I had no idea what she said, but she sounded excited."

Grace laughed. "Not what they were expecting, huh?"

"No. Ethan isn't as traditional as they are, and I didn't know anything about Greek culture until I met him. But when I was in Greece, I fell in love with his family. Their customs should be treasured, and I want to pass them down to our children one day."

"There you go again, talking about kids." Her lungs burned as she spoke. "Just remember, your whole life changes once you have a baby."

"I know, I know. But Ethan and I will make a good team. He'll be such a good dad."

Grace stopped for a moment to catch her breath. It would've been much different raising Liam if she'd had a significant other by her side. A husband who could've helped with diaper changes and feedings in the middle of the night. A stepdad who could've consoled Liam when she couldn't get him to stop crying. A man who could've poured her a warm bath to relax in when she needed a break.

Heck, having a significant other would be nice even now. To help her figure out what was going on with Liam lately and navigate his teen years. But she'd made it through those tough early years as a single mom, and she could do it in the years to come.

Up ahead, Amanda jogged in place. "What are you doing? We've only gone a mile."

"Only one? Are you sure? I think your watch is broken."

"Come on, slow poke. I need to stay in shape before my big day."

"I don't remember agreeing to be your exercise buddy when I said I'd be your maid of honor."

Amanda flashed a grin. "It was an unspoken agreement."

She put her hands on her hips. "No signature, no contract."

"Stop stalling and get moving, Cunningham."

"Ugh, fine." She ran to catch up with her friend. "You have to understand, I don't have the same motivation to get in shape like you do. It's not like anyone will be looking at me. They'll all be staring at you."

"Not everyone. I'm sure my brother's eyes will be focused on someone else."

Her cheeks flushed with warmth, more from Amanda's words than the exercise. "Let's get back to party planning. Now that we've taken care of your bridal shower invites, what do you want to do for your bachelorette party?"

"Ethan and I want to do a joint party. We'd love to do something outside."

"That's a good idea. Let me think." The longer she ran, the harder she had to work at keeping conversation. "We could go on the River Boat Cruise. Didn't you and Ethan do that when you first met?"

"I've thought about that too, but I'd like to do something more active."

"Of course, you would." She kept her tone light.

"How about tubing or canoeing?"

"I hadn't thought about either of those. Definite possibilities." Amanda glanced at the Orick Hills strip mall as they ran past a group of teenagers hanging out in the parking lot. "I'd like to have the party one of the first weekends of June, and my only worry is that the water is still cold then."

"There must be something we haven't thought of yet. Something you've always wanted to do with Ethan."

Amanda stopped. "Wait, I've got it. Ethan and I have always talked about going to the Mystical Caves. We could go hiking and then go out to a brewery for dinner and drinks afterward."

The Mystical Caves. Grace hadn't thought about those caves in years, but the memories she had of them still made her knees weak. She needed to keep moving before they gave out entirely. She jogged forward, tugging on Amanda to keep going.

"Uh, why the sudden interest in our run?"

"No reason."

Amanda glanced at Grace, her eyes growing wide. "Oh, I know. That's where you and Caleb almost …"

She nodded. One summer afternoon, they'd hiked through the caves alone and found the darkest cave. They spent the next few hours kissing, getting lost in one another, and losing all track of time. "So, any other ideas? I'm sure we could think of more places."

Amanda grinned. "Nope. I think the caves are perfect."

"Right. Okay." She gave a curt nod. Amanda was the bride, and if she wanted to go hiking, then that was what they'd do. "What if we added an extra element to hiking?"

"Like what?"

"Something competitive." She blew out a relieved breath as they rounded the sidewalk and turned onto the same street as Cedar Crest. Only a few more blocks to go. "We could split into teams and have a scavenger hunt."

"I like it. We could write everyone's names on popsicle sticks. Ethan and I could be the team captains and pick sticks when we get to the park."

"Perfect." At least if they split into teams, she had a fifty-fifty chance of being on a different team than Caleb. She could only hope.

Because being in the caves with him, remembering what almost happened that day, would not erase her growing attraction to him.

❧

CALEB PUT HIS hand on his forehead, blocking out the sun as he scanned the bleachers. After a minute, he caught sight of Grace and her mom sitting in the middle row. Grace wore a baseball cap, Mustangs T-shirt, and athletic shorts.

Wow. She had to be the most attractive mom sitting in the stands. Ignoring the way his heart picked up speed, he walked toward her, waving as he drew near.

She slid over to make space for him, a slight smile playing on her lips. "I didn't know you were coming."

"Liam invited me."

"Oh." Her smile faltered.

Did it bother her that Liam had invited him? Or was she upset about pretending to be Amanda and Ethan at the bakery?

She couldn't be *that* mad. She'd seemed to enjoy it just as much as he had.

A week had gone by since that afternoon, and he couldn't stop thinking about it. Despite his allergic reaction, it was one of the best days he'd had in a long time. On his own, he brooded about what to do with his life. Sitting next to her, he could be present in the moment, laughing and enjoying the easy banter.

The best part was when she ran back into the bakery with his EpiPen. She stared at him for several seconds. Probably the whole place had, but he caught the look in her eyes. Attraction. Longing.

She wanted to kiss him.

He had to admit, the same thought had crossed his mind more than once. Not that he would do anything about it.

A little girl in a red, white, and blue dress waltzed out to the middle of the field.

The announcer's voice bellowed over the loudspeaker. "Please stand for our nation anthem."

Standing, he put his hand over his heart. He'd heard this song every day for the last eleven years, but he still managed to fumble the words. Mostly because he could never focus on the words. Instead, images of war resurfaced—the people he hadn't saved, the flag-covered body bags, the caskets being lowered into the ground. Those images haunted his dreams.

The little girl's voice rose an octave higher as she held the last note.

Grace turned to look at him, her eyes filled with compassion. She reached for his hand and intertwined their fingers.

His lips parted. Despite the years they'd spent apart, she still seemed to notice his uneasiness, as if she could detect the torment he held within and the memories that scratched at his insides.

The teams and parents clapped in praise. Grace let go of his hand, put two fingers in her mouth, and let out a loud whistle. "Go Mustangs!"

He had the unexpected urge to pull her hand back. Instead, he sat down next to her, glanced at the dugout, and shouted, "Go get 'em, Liam."

The boy looked up, a slow, nervous grin spreading across his face.

Mrs. Cunningham shifted on the bleachers as she ran manicured fingers through her reddish-brown bangs. A few seconds later, she made a quiet *tsk* noise.

Grace drew her attention away from the field. "What was that for?"

"It's just a game. I'll never understand why people take sports so seriously. It puts too much pressure on kids."

"Maybe you should go back to the house and get some sleep, Mom. You're tired, and to be honest with you, you're a little cranky today."

Mrs. Cunningham crossed her legs. "I can't believe you said that to me. I've never missed one of Liam's games. I'm not about to start now."

"I wasn't trying to upset you."

"Well, I wouldn't be so tired if the rain hadn't leaked into Mr. Gardner's room and woken him up. That hailstorm must've damaged our roof."

Caleb leaned forward, making eye contact with Mrs. Cunningham. "I can call one of my buddies. He works for a siding and roofing company. I'm sure he'd give you a fair price to repair it."

"Oh. Um, sure. That would be nice."

"If you have any other repairs around Cedar Crest, I'd be happy to help while I'm staying there."

Grace nudged her elbow into his side. "Are you sure you want to open that can of worms?"

"Yup. Consider the can opened." As he spoke, Liam's coach prepped the team before the upcoming inning. He paced back and forth in the dugout, his voice growing loud with enthusiasm.

Grace's phone rang, quietly playing a classic tune. "Hello?" She paused, then cupped her hand over the receiver. "It's your sister. I'll be right back." She moved off the bleachers and stood a few feet away.

The opposing team spread out on the field. On the pitcher's mound, a gangly kid dug his cleats into the ground and licked his lips.

Davis sauntered up to home plate, seemingly unperturbed. He bent his knees, leaned forward, and gripped the bat.

Mrs. Cunningham perched on the edge of the metal seat. "Davis has a lot of potential. I'm excited he's on our team for the last few games of the season."

"I've seen him and Liam practicing a lot in the backyard. Have they been friends for a while?"

"No, they met when Davis and his mom came to stay at the bed-and-breakfast. I'm so happy they're friends. Liam had good friends in Missouri, but after we moved to Iowa, he's had a hard time making new ones."

Caleb frowned. Why wouldn't anyone want to be friends with Liam?

On the field, Davis missed the pitch. He let out a curse word, loud enough for the parents in the stands to hear.

The coach cupped his hands around his mouth. "Davis, calm down and focus."

Caleb held his breath as Davis missed the next two consecutive pitches. *Bummer.*

Davis lifted the bat, then slammed it against the ground over and over. Orange dust flew up from the field and landed on his white pants.

The coach jogged over and yanked the bat out of Davis's hand, then pulled the kid aside.

A woman shot up from her seat in the stands. Her cheeks turned bright red as she clutched her purse and walked toward Davis and the coach.

She must be Davis's mom. Had he met her before? She looked oddly familiar. Before he could think about it for too long, Grace returned to her seat and the game resumed.

Two hours later, Liam skipped over to the stands with a big grin on his face. He'd scored the last run of the game, making the final score 10 to 6. "The team wants to go out for pizza and ice cream to celebrate our win. Can we go, Mom?"

"Of course. An ice cream sundae sounds amazing after sitting out here in this heat."

Liam glanced at Caleb. "Wanna come too?"

"I'd love to." He exchanged a look with Grace. "If it's okay with your mom, that is."

She bit her bottom lip. "Sure."

Mrs. Cunningham rubbed her temples. "I'll sit this one out. I'm tired, as you reminded me earlier. I'd like to go home and close my eyes for a bit."

"You and Liam can ride with me," Caleb offered.

At Happy Joe's Pizza, the team took over a long, rectangular table in the middle of the restaurant. Their boisterous laughter rose above the conversations at nearby booths, where families sat enjoying dinners of their own.

As soon as the waitress dropped off their pizza, Grace unraveled her silverware from the napkin and picked up the fork.

Caleb reached for a piece of pepperoni. "Don't tell me you're one of those people who eats pizza with a fork."

"What's wrong with that?" she asked.

"It's pizza." He wiggled his fingers. "It's meant to be eaten with your hands."

"Says who?"

"Says me." Smirking, he took a big bite. Red sauce oozed onto his chin.

She grinned and handed him a napkin. "Point proven." Using her fork, she cut into her pizza and took a small bite. "On a more serious note, I meant to ask you earlier, what was all that yelling I heard when I was on the phone?"

"Davis struck out. He got angry and started hitting the ground with his bat."

"Wow. I've never seen him behave that way."

Caleb dipped his pizza in ranch. "Yeah, it escalated quickly. Do you know why he'd be so angry? Besides the game, I mean."

She took a sip of lemonade from her straw. "I've spoken with his mom a few times at breakfast. His parents just got divorced, and Davis has had a hard time adjusting. His mom won sole legal custody, and he'd rather live with his dad."

"Is his dad still in the picture?"

"Yeah, he has visitation rights. In fact, Liam asked me if he could spend the night at Davis's dad's house the day of the bachelor and bachelorette party. His dad's house isn't too far away from Cedar Crest."

Caleb scratched the back of his head. "Do you think that's a good idea?"

"Why are you questioning me on this?" She put down her fork.

Shoot. He'd offended her. "Liam is a good kid who could easily get influenced by a kid like Davis."

"I agree, but I've also seen how kind Davis is. He's offered to help me around the bed-and-breakfast on several occasions."

"I see."

"Plus, I'll meet Davis's dad before the sleepover. If I don't feel comfortable, I won't let Liam stay there."

"Okay." Was this what it felt like to have a kid, to want to protect their every move? To keep them safe? He reached across the table and put his hand on her cheek. "I shouldn't have questioned you. You're a good mom."

"Thank you." She noticeably swallowed at his touch.

Her reaction weaved warmth around his heart. Somehow, in the last few months, he'd started to care about Grace and Liam.

How had he let this happen? This wasn't part of his plan. Sooner or later, he would move back to Maple Valley or reenlist. And after that, Grace and Liam would move on with their lives, without him.

An unexpected ache tugged at his chest. They didn't need a third person to complete their perfect duo.

Chapter 8

GRACE OPENED THE oven door and pulled out the charred cherry pie. Smoke spiraled all around her, stinging her nostrils. She turned on the ceiling fan to air out the kitchen. Not the best way to start a Monday morning. Was the oven repairable or broken for good? She'd have to call an electrician to find out for sure.

A laugh bubbled in her throat because if she didn't laugh, she'd cry.

"What happened?" Caleb walked into the kitchen, wearing shorts and a camo T-shirt that fit snugly around his biceps.

"I was baking a pie, and the oven started smoking. I turned it off as soon I smelled the burnt crust." She yanked the oven mitt off her hand and tossed it on the counter. "It's one broken thing after the next. This place is a money pit."

"You need a break. Which is perfect because I came down to see if you'd want to go out for that day of fun that I promised you."

She shook her head. "I have a million things to do. First and foremost, I need to get a hold of an electrician."

"You have *a million* things to do?"

"Maybe not a million, but stuff that should get done today."

He smirked, making the dimple in his cheek more pronounced. "Now you're changing the story. Call an electrician and then meet me outside in fifteen minutes. You won't be gone all day, and you can finish that to-do list of yours when you get home."

She bit her bottom lip. Getting away for a while *did* sound nice. Mom could let the electrician in and the rest of the chores could get done later. "Okay."

"Great." He rubbed his hands together, a mischievous spark lighting in his sky-blue eyes.

"I don't like that look. Where are we going?"

"I'll put it this way; I'm willing to bet it's something different from anything you've done before."

He had that right. His something different was a helicopter ride. An hour after their conversation, she sat in the parked aircraft, her stomach doing flip-flops at the thought of going up hundreds of feet in this thing. "I'm afraid of heights."

Caleb took her hand and squeezed it. "Think of this as 'me time.' You work hard. You deserve to have a little—"

"Fun," she finished. "So, you say, but I'm beginning

to realize your idea of fun and my idea of fun are not the same."

He laughed—a rich husky sound that soothed her nerves.

"Let's go before I jump out." Her heart raced as she buckled her seat belt.

Grinning, he pressed several buttons on the console. The engine purred to life. He handed her large padded headphones. "Put these on."

She adjusted them over her ears as the aircraft vibrated, then rose into the sky. She clutched the sides of her seat. Her stomach somersaulted. How had she let him talk her into this?

He glanced over at her and winked. "Stop worrying and look down."

Look down? She swallowed hard and glanced out the window. Lush green farmland stretched as far as she could see. Little specks of black, brown, and white dotted the ground. "Are those cows and horses?"

"Yup."

The helicopter rose higher until the specks disappeared and dark blue water snaked through the farmland. "There's the Mississippi River."

"It looks pretty harmless from all the way up here, doesn't it?"

She nodded and rested her head against the back of her seat. What a view. A calming peace washed over her, erasing the anxious adrenaline from before. She glanced over at Caleb.

He gripped the console so hard his knuckles were white. His face held a similar ashen color.

Oh no. Just when she was starting to feel comfortable. "What's wrong?"

His Adam's apple bobbed up and down. He squeezed his eyes shut for a moment, then opened them.

"Did you forget to put enough gas in? Are we going to crash?"

Caleb slowly inhaled and exhaled. "I didn't mean to scare you. I just had a flashback."

"From one of your missions?"

"Yeah. The memory flashed before my eyes. It came out of nowhere."

Her chest constricted. She couldn't imagine the hardships he'd endured during his time in the service. Part of her didn't want to know the details, but it would help him to talk about his experiences. "What did you just remember?"

His shoulders noticeably tensed. "One night early in my career, I landed the aircraft in a hot landing zone that was compromised with agricultural rows."

"What does that mean?" she asked quietly.

"We were being shot at, but we couldn't see where the enemy was because they were hiding behind rows of crops. We were there to pick up a soldier who had stepped on an IED. The explosive device had opened his stomach cavity. When my crew carried him to the helicopter, some of his insides fell out." He flinched as if he could still see it. "It was the most horrendous scene I ever encountered."

Grace sucked in a breath, trying to keep her composure. She put her hand on his cheek. "That's terrible."

He leaned into her touch. "What I remember most—aside from seeing how white our bones really are—is that the injured soldier had a wedding ring on. Once we had him safely in the aircraft, I couldn't stop thinking about his wife. How she would most likely be a widow."

"If that was one of your earlier missions, how did you keep going after that?"

"Once you've tasted combat, taken enemy fire, and ripped men and women from the arms of death, you only want more. Combat was the most addictive experience of my life. That's why I've gone back over and over again. I want the rush, the satisfaction. I want to make a difference." He sighed. "Let's talk about something else. I promised you a fun time, and I intend on keeping my promise."

Despite the beautiful view below, she couldn't look away from Caleb. Back in high school, she'd never seen this vulnerable side of him. Not even after his mom died.

His raw honesty showed how much he'd changed

and how much he'd endured since the air force. How selfless he was to serve and protect the United States. How brave he was to risk his life by flying into dangerous situations to save others.

She'd never regretted leaving Maple Valley and starting over. But the more time she spent with Caleb, the more she second-guessed her decision to break up with him. He'd turned out to be one of the most remarkable and respectable men she'd ever met.

CALEB LICKED HIS lips as Grace set several pieces of blueberry pie on the dining room table. Steam rose from the pie, and the sweet, sugary scent of blueberries floated through the room.

She set a plate in front of Mayor Jennings. "There's also a pot of decaf coffee just around the corner if anyone wants a cup during your meeting."

"Great." Jennings cut into the pie with his fork. Blueberries oozed onto his plate. "I appreciate you letting us meet here and making the pie. It looks delicious."

"My pleasure. I love baking." She wiped her hands on the apron tied around her slim waist. "When my oven's working, that is."

Caleb met her gaze across the table. "That's great that the electrician fixed it, and you didn't have to buy a new one."

She crossed her fingers. "Let's just hope it stays working." She scanned the crowded table. "If there's anything else you need, I'll be in the living room."

"Thanks, Grace." Jennings swallowed a bite of pie and turned his attention to the committee. "I'm glad you're all here tonight. Your input is invaluable, and I truly believe we can make Maple Valley better than it ever was before."

Caleb leaned forward, resting his elbows on the table. Time to find out what Jennings had in mind. What would the town look like when it was done? Which stores would stay, and which ones would go?

The mayor clasped his hands together. "I'll start with the good news. The governor issued a disaster proclamation. We'll get both state and federal money to help with our remodel."

Affirmative responses circulated around the table.

"One of the biggest changes Knox would like to make is to elevate the ground between the river and the downtown area. As I'm sure you can guess, creating a hill will decrease the likelihood of a flood hitting us as hard as it did."

Caleb nodded. "Makes sense."

"The rest of the money will be spent remodeling the houses and stores hit by the flood." Jennings stroked his beard. "This is where it could get difficult. I'm hoping each owner will sell their property to Mt. Point Development. Once this is taken care of, we'll pick which stores will stay."

Dad and Sandy exchanged nervous glances. "What if I don't want to sell the Canine Palace?" Dad asked.

"Mr. Meyers—"

Dad slapped his palm on the table. "We've known each other for twenty years, *Beauford*. Call me Ray."

"S-Sorry." The mayor's cheeks turned a dark reddish hue. "Look, I don't want to do this, but if anyone refuses to sell, we can use eminent domain."

Caleb cocked his head to the side. "What does that mean, exactly?"

"We could force owners to sell. The municipality of Maple Valley would condemn each property, buy them, and sell them to Mt. Point Development."

Valerie's fork clattered to her plate. "That doesn't seem right. I should have the freedom to make my own decision about Val's Diner."

"I understand where you're coming from, but you're only considering what's best for you," Jennings said. "I have to do what's best for this town. It would be better, and less expensive, if Knox owned every property in the downtown area. That way, he could start with a fresh slate instead of working around some of the buildings."

Caleb steepled his fingers beneath his chin. "I thought you wanted our input."

Jennings stared at him for a moment. "I'd like to move forward with the town's support. The best chance we have of gaining their support is if we're united. I'm asking those of you who are business owners to be the first to sell. Start the trend and show other owners you're on board with the plan."

Dad rose from his seat. "What's the point of being on this committee if we don't get a say?"

"You will."

"Forget it. I'll wait for you on the porch, Sandy." Shaking his head, Dad marched out of the dining room. The door slammed behind him.

His eyebrows rose. *Was it the heightened circumstances, or was Dad getting feistier in his old age?* He would talk to him after the meeting. Try to calm him down.

"That's all I have for this meeting." The mayor's shoulders sagged. "I'll get in touch with each of you soon."

Caleb scrubbed a hand over his face. He had to agree with Valerie. It wasn't right for Jennings to force owners to sell or even threaten to do it.

If *he* was the mayor, he wouldn't put people in that position. He would give them the facts and show them why it was a good idea to sell, then give them the choice. If they didn't want to sell, *he* would tell Mr. Bennett to figure out a way to make the plan work. Most importantly, *he* would make Maple Valley citizens his first priority.

Pushing those thoughts aside, Caleb walked into the living room. Sandy stood with some of the committee members, their frustrated whispers almost loud enough to hear. *Good.* If she was still here, then Dad was too.

He opened the door and stepped out onto the porch, where Dad sat in a plastic lawn chair. The smell of charcoal and smoke mingled with the scent of freshly mowed grass—a sign that summer was almost here.

"Some meeting, huh?" Dad crossed his arms. "Beauford has lost his mind. I would never sell the Canine Palace to a developer."

"I get it. I wouldn't want to either." Caleb leaned against the short brick wall surrounding the edge of the porch. "Do you think Jennings is serious about eminent domain?"

"I hope not. One of things that kept me going when I had cancer was thinking about the Canine Palace. I was excited to go back to work full time and see all my customers." Dad bent his leg and rested it above his other knee. "I'm not starting all over again."

He nodded in understanding. Owning the Canine Palace had brought Dad back to life. It gave him a new purpose, a way to move on after Mom's death. It gave him a reason to fight for his own life when cancer threatened to take it away. "I'll figure something out. I won't let him take it away from you."

Behind thick glasses, Dad's eyes glistened. "Have I

told you how glad I am that you're home, son?"

Caleb gave a weak smile. What would Dad say if he knew Caleb had considered reenlisting? Would he be supportive, or would he try to talk him out of it? "I need to be honest with you. I'm not sure I'll stay. I miss being in the air force."

A few seconds passed before Dad responded. "You want to go back?"

"Possibly. I miss the rush and sense of purpose I had while saving lives, or even saving soldiers who had already died, so their families could have closure." He crossed one ankle in front of the other. "But I like being home with you and Amanda too. Seeing you whenever I want, being a part of all the wedding plans … it's nice."

"If you want my opinion, I would give it time. When I got back from Vietnam, it took years until I felt whole again."

Was that the problem? Could time mend the broken pieces of his soul? Or was he forever stained by death and war?

❧

LATER THAT NIGHT, Caleb shut the door to his room and grabbed Seth's box out of the closet. After talking to his dad, he had the unexpected urge to call Seth and ask for his opinion.

Man, what he wouldn't do to talk to his best friend again.

Expelling a deep breath, Caleb opened the box. He picked up several items: pilot wings, a picture of them smoking cigars after a mission, Seth's recipe for his famous smoked brisket, and their high school yearbook.

Caleb wiped his hand across the yearbook, cleaning off layers of dust. He flipped through pages of pictures. Classmates with bad haircuts, pimple-covered foreheads, and ridiculous clothing styles. Halfway through the thick book, a picture and an envelope fell out and drifted under the bed.

He picked up the photo. It was a picture taken at prom. Caleb, Grace, Seth, and Amanda stood in the front row of a big group wearing formal dresses and tuxedos.

Grace looked stunning in a sleeveless lavender dress that flowed down to her ankles. She wore diamond-studded earrings, his mom's pearl necklace, and light touches of makeup that showcased her long eyelashes. Right before they'd walked out the door, Dad had stopped them, carrying two of his mom's necklaces—one for Grace to borrow and one for Amanda.

He smiled. There were fifteen people in the picture, all of them squished together so no one would be cut out. Grace was sandwiched between Caleb and Seth. Caleb had his arm draped across Grace's shoulders, and

Seth's hand was so close to hers that it almost looked like he was trying to hold her hand.

Weird. He'd never noticed that before.

He placed the photo inside the box and continued looking through the yearbook. Everyone looked so young. What he'd give to go back to those carefree days, when his biggest problem was what cafeteria food to eat for lunch or competing in the baseball state championship.

Now he was knee-deep in problems. Should he reenlist? Should he stay to fight for the town he loved? If Mt. Point Development got their way, the historical atmosphere he'd always enjoyed would be gone, replaced with evenly paved streets, perfectly measured landscaping, and freshly painted siding.

The memories he cherished from Maple Valley—playing tag with friends in the school park, eating at Val's Diner with Grace, even sitting at the table by the window in Candy Galore where his parents met—would forever be changed.

He closed the yearbook. Then again, he could always make new memories. Like pretending to be a bride and groom at the bakery. Or flying a helicopter over nearby farmland and watching Grace as the beauty of flying overcame her fear.

Maybe *new* wasn't all bad. Maybe he needed to be more open-minded. Because his closed-off heart was opening up and letting Grace in bit by bit. Spending time with her made him realize how lonely he'd been.

He shook his head. What was he thinking? Alone was all he knew. He wasn't cut out for a serious relationship.

Chapter 9

THE FOLLOWING WEEKEND, Grace stood at the entrance of Mystic Caves Park. She reached into the open jar and mixed the folded slips of paper. "Our bride and groom are the team captains. Once the teams are chosen, we'll hike separately and search for the scavenger hunt items. Each team should take pictures to prove you found the items on the list."

Amanda pumped her fist in the air. "We're totally going to win."

Ethan chuckled. "Maybe you should wait to talk smack until you know who's on your team."

"I don't need to wait. I have a good feeling."

Grace handed her friend the jar. "You get to pick first."

Amanda pulled out a slip of paper and unfolded it. "Kendall."

"Yay." Kendall stepped away from the small group and stood next to Amanda.

"My turn." Ethan pulled out a piece of paper, smirking. "Cole."

Cole smiled as he moved beside his cousin.

Amanda laughed. "Next on my team is … Grace."

"Woo-hoo." She moved next to Kendall, excitement bubbling in her chest. She needed this. An entire day away from Cedar Crest with no responsibilities other than making sure Amanda and Ethan enjoyed themselves.

And making sure she kept her thoughts in check. No thinking about the past or what had almost happened here. She snuck a quick peek at Caleb. He wore athletic shorts that showed off his well-defined calves, a black shirt that clung to his sculpted chest, and a North Face backpack.

Heat rose up the back of her neck. She looked away from him and focused on Amanda and Ethan as they continued taking turns.

Ethan randomly chose his friend from the oncology unit at Furnam Hospital and one of Amanda's nurses from the birthing center. Amanda chose Ethan's teenage cousin. Only two people remained—Caleb and Charlie.

"This is it." Amanda grinned. "Please not my brother. Please not my brother."

Grace bit her bottom lip. *I second that.*

Amanda unfolded the paper, pretending to pout. "Caleb."

"Trust me, by the end of the day, you'll be happy I

was on your team." As he spoke, he looked at Grace and winked.

Ugh. Leaving the teams up to chance was a bad idea. "Let's go."

As they hiked, Grace inhaled the sweet, fresh scents of nature. Sunlight shone through the green canopy, warming her face. Birds flitted from one tree to the next, singing high-pitched melodies. This was nice. She should go hiking more often.

Several trails weaved around Orick Hills and surrounding towns, which was why she thought it would be a good location for a bed-and-breakfast. But she hadn't had much time to hike. Maybe she would have more time after Amanda's wedding and then she could bring Liam.

Hopefully, he was having fun with Davis today and staying safe. She'd met Davis's dad this morning, and he seemed like a good guy. He told the boys they could cook s'mores by a bonfire when it got dark. Liam would love that.

She glanced up. A rock the size of a minivan sat on top of a rock less than half its size. She stopped hiking and pointed. "Is that Balanced Rock?"

Caleb glanced at the map in her hands. "Yup. Looks like it."

Amanda took a picture with her cell phone and crossed off the item on the scavenger hunt paper. "Next is Natural Bridge. I think it's that way."

Grace followed Amanda's gaze as her friend pointed to a narrow trail awash with color. Wildflowers and prairie clovers painted the woods with splashes of yellow and purple. Tall maples and oaks towered overhead, their long thick branches stooping in different directions.

Caleb gestured for Amanda to lead the way. Grace and Kendall walked side by side with Ethan's cousin, Harold, pulling up the rear.

In front of her, Caleb's head moved slowly from one side of the woods to the other, taking it all in. He latched his thumbs beneath the shoulder straps of his backpack, whistling.

She smiled. He was in his element. After seeing how strongly his post-traumatic stress had affected him during the helicopter ride, it was nice to see him so relaxed.

"I found Natural Bridge." Kendall stopped and peered at a large rock formation shaped like a half circle. Each side of the circle connected to the trail up above with a missing gap of land underneath. Plants and grass had grown over the curved rock and weeds hung over the edge.

Amanda turned to Caleb. "Remember when dad took us to this spot and you ran ahead of me, hid under that bridge, and popped out, trying to scare me?"

He laughed. "*Trying* to scare you? I think you had to change your pants after I jumped out at you."

Amanda picked up a stick and poked him with it. "Did not."

"Did too," he said.

Grace put her hands on her hips and used her best stern voice. "Now, now, you two. Let's not fight."

Caleb nudged her ribs with his elbow, sending an electric charge shooting through her. "Oh, come on, Mom. Amanda started it."

Grace shook her head, trying to ignore the sensation. A smile tugged at her lips. She'd forgotten how easy it was to laugh and joke with Caleb and Amanda. She'd forgotten what it felt like to be a part of their family.

Harold ran up the hill, his gangly arms propelling him up to the top of the bridge. "Will one of you take my picture?"

Caleb jogged up the hill as well. He put his hands on his hips and puffed out his chest, looking like Superman. The movement caused his T-shirt to lift, exposing hard, lean abs.

Whoa. A decade in the air force had really sculpted his body. She forced her gaze away and reached for her cell to take a picture.

"Thanks," Harold said. "Let's find Dancehall Cave next."

"You got it." Caleb turned toward a new trail, leading the way.

She couldn't help noticing how his athletic shorts fit

snugly around his butt. With every exposed part of him being muscular, surely, his butt was all muscle too.

Beside her, Amanda lifted her eyebrows.

Grace glared at her friend. "Shut up," she whispered.

"I didn't say anything."

"You didn't have to."

Amanda laughed and looped her arm around Grace's.

Twenty feet ahead, steep muddy stairs descended into the mouth of a dark cave.

"Be careful. It's slippery." Caleb unzipped his backpack, grabbed a headlamp, and adjusted it over his blond hair. "There are LED lights throughout the cave, but I'll wear this just in case it's not lit enough."

Amanda snorted. "We'll be fine. We've been through these caves hundreds of times."

"We have, but not everybody else has."

Rolling her eyes at their banter, Grace stepped into the mouth of the cave. She carefully moved along a narrow sidewalk that was built a few inches above a stream. The farther they walked, the deeper the stream became.

Caleb stopped and pointed to the muddy sidewalk. "I see footprints."

"Me too." Amanda groaned. "That means Ethan's team has already been here. We need to hurry. I want bragging rights, people."

"Aye, Captain." Chuckling, Caleb trekked through the wet mud at a faster pace.

Grace tried to keep up with him by focusing her gaze on her feet and praying she didn't face-plant in the mud. They hadn't planned on changing their clothes before going to the brewery tonight.

A couple feet ahead of her, Caleb mumbled something incoherent.

She glanced up to see his large form tilting to one side of the path, then he fell in the water. A loud splash echoed through the quiet cave.

She carefully sped over to the spot where he'd fallen. "Are you okay?"

He sat up in the water, shaking his head like a wet dog. His headlamp hung loosely over one ear. Sucking in a breath, he leaned forward and reached for his ankle.

"What's wrong?" she asked.

"I think I twisted it."

"I'm so sorry that I made you hurry," Amanda said.

"Who wants to carry me out?" He kept his tone light, but there was an edge to his voice.

Grace exchanged glances with her teammates, frowning as she realized none of them could lift Caleb. He had to be at least two hundred pounds. She pulled out her cell phone and glanced at the home screen. "No service."

"We'll have to find Ethan's team." Amanda put her hands on her hips. "I'm sure they can carry Caleb out."

Harold stepped down into the water and extended his arm. "Sorry that I can't carry you out, man. But I can get you out of the water."

"Thanks." Wincing, Caleb grabbed Harold's hand and let Harold pull him up. Once he stood, he hobbled to the sidewalk and sat down.

Amanda squeezed her brother's shoulder. "We'll hurry as fast as we can. Do you want someone to stay with you?"

"Nah, I'll be fine."

"I'll stay with you." Grace said it without thinking. She couldn't let him sit alone in a cave with a twisted ankle. That was the only reason she'd said it.

Caleb nodded without looking at her.

Amanda, Kendall, and Harold walked back toward the entrance of the cave. The sound of their footsteps slowly faded away, replaced with a quiet and rhythmic *drip, drip, drip*.

Caleb leaned back on his hands. "This brings back memories."

"Yup." Her response came out sharp and rushed. They shouldn't be talking about the last time they'd been alone in a cave. She needed to make small talk and turn this conversation around. "I'm glad the weather is turning warmer. June is my favorite month of the year."

He laughed. "You want to talk about the weather?"

"It's better than thinking about the last time we were

in a cave together." Shivering, she pulled her knees up to her chest and wrapped her arms around her legs.

"Are you cold?"

"A little." Wearing a T-shirt and shorts had kept her warm while they were hiking, but it had to be at least ten degrees cooler inside the cave.

"Come here."

She hesitated. Being any closer to Caleb seemed like a bad idea, but if she didn't warm up soon, she wouldn't be able to sit here with him. She scooted over to his side. Despite his wet clothes, heat radiated from his body.

He rested his arm around her shoulders. "Can I ask you a personal question?"

"Sure …"

"How come you never came back to Maple Valley, or called me to let me know what happened to you?"

"I thought about it. But I always came to the same conclusion. I didn't think you'd understand my choices."

He turned toward her slightly and put his hand under her chin, lifting it. "Now that I know what happened, I do understand. As much I can without going through it myself, anyway. And I fully commend you for keeping and raising Liam by yourself. That must've been a tough decision."

She snuggled closer. She didn't need anyone else to respect her choices, but it was nice to hear his words of affirmation.

"I know I've told you this before, and I'll say it again. You're a great mom." He glanced down at her lips, then looked away. "But I think you should date more often. I can tell you're running on empty."

Her heart picked up speed.

He looked at her lips again, this time his gaze unwavering. "You deserve to have your tank filled up."

What a sweet thing to say. Her chest swelled. He *did* still care about her. Casting all her fears aside, she tilted her head and broke the space between them. Her lips brushed against his in a gentle kiss.

Shifting, he moved his hands through the depths of her hair, pulling her closer for a deeper, passionate kiss.

She wrapped her arms around his neck, relishing in the woodsy scent of his skin. Her body melted into his, and she could feel the pounding of his heart, beating like a fast, steady drum.

He pulled his lips away from hers as he trailed slow kisses down her neck.

She gave a throaty sigh. Tingles shot up and down her spine. *Is this what I've been missing all these years?* Electric chemistry spread from her lips to her toes, igniting a sudden and aching longing.

He brought his lips to hers again as heavy footsteps approached.

She jerked away, putting space between them.

Ethan smirked. "Amanda told me to hurry, but I can

see you two found a way to occupy yourselves."

Caleb chuckled.

What had she just done? Kissing Caleb when they had no intentions of dating was cruel. If they weren't careful, one or both of them would get hurt. *Again*.

❦

THE LEAVES CRUNCHED beneath Liam's feet as he stepped into the woods. "Are you sure we should be out here? Alone, I mean."

Davis shrugged. "Yeah, my dad lets me go wherever I want."

"Even at night?"

Davis stopped walking and put his hands on his hips. "What? Are you chicken or somethin'?"

A lump lodged in Liam's throat. "No."

"Good. 'Cause if we want a big bonfire, we need a lot of sticks." Davis maneuvered through the thickening woods.

Liam tried to swallow the lump in his throat, but it wouldn't budge. How much was "a lot"? He had to focus his attention on something else. Something more positive. At least summer was finally here. Two whole months without his classmates. Two whole months without hearing them laugh at him when the teacher wasn't paying attention.

An owl hooted from one of the nearby trees. He glanced up but couldn't see it. The fading sunlight had darkened the sky. A shiver ran down his spine. He walked quickly, picking up as many sticks as he could and cradling the growing bundle in his arms. He had to pretend he wasn't scared, especially in front of Davis, who didn't seem afraid at all.

After what seemed like an eternity, Davis directed them out of the woods and into his dad's backyard. A stone-encased firepit sat in the middle of the lawn with four wooden benches surrounding it.

He dropped his collection of sticks beside the firepit and sat down on a bench.

Bending over the pit, Davis ripped newspapers apart and threw them in. He arranged the sticks and a few logs that had already been placed near the firepit, and then lit the paper with a lighter. Little flames flickered to life. He blew on the flames until they grew taller and started burning the wood.

"How do you know how to make a fire?" Liam asked.

"My dad taught me. We used to go camping a lot."

Liam leaned forward, resting his elbows on his knees. He frowned. "I've never been camping."

Davis moved to the bench across from him. "We had a motor home, so we went lots of places."

"Where is it?"

"We don't have it anymore. My dad had to sell it when my parents got divorced. Guess he needed child support money or something like that."

"How come your parents got divorced?"

Davis stood and adjusted the bigger logs, shifting them to the middle of the pit. Light from the flames flickered across his downturned face. "It's my mom's fault. She's the one who wanted a divorce. She was always complaining about my dad. Now, I only get to see him every other weekend."

Liam dug his shoe into the grass. It sounded like Davis really missed his dad. Heck, even in the short time Liam had known Caleb, he would miss him if he left.

Mom said he might go back to the air force, which would suck. Caleb was a cool guy. In his free time, he built Legos with Liam, he helped Mom with broken stuff at the bed-and-breakfast, and best of all, he made Mom laugh.

"Hey, do you want to see something?" The growing flames lit the excitement in Davis's eyes.

"Sure." He followed Davis to the side of the house.

Davis pulled a flashlight out of the pocket of his baggy shorts and directed the light to two old doors in the ground.

Liam wrinkled his nose. "What are doors doing in the ground?"

"It's a storm shelter. People use them during tornados and stuff." Davis pulled back one of the doors and climbed inside. "Come on."

He stayed rooted in place, peering into the opening as Davis walked down a short flight of stairs. "Where are you going?"

Davis disappeared into the darkness for a moment, then walked back to the opening and unclenched his fist to show Liam what was in his hand. "How cool is this?"

"I can't see it very well. What is it?"

Davis shined the flashlight on his hand. "A firework. The whole shelter is full of them. The old owners must've forgotten about the box when they moved." A slow, wide smile spread across his face, like the Cheshire cat in *Alice's Adventures in Wonderland*. "Want to light them with me sometime?"

"Uh, I don't know."

"Trust me, it's a lot of fun."

"You've done it before?"

"Yup. A couple times." Davis stuffed a handful of fireworks in his pocket. "Soon, I plan to light a whole bunch of them at the same time. The fire will be huge."

"Wow," Liam said, pretending to be astonished. But deep down, his gut hardened. Should he tell Mom about this? It seemed dangerous.

And yet, if he tattled, Davis wouldn't want to be his friend anymore. Maybe he could try to talk Davis out of it when the time came.

❦

"Thank you." Caleb took the warm mug from Grace and cupped his hands around it. Taking a sip, he eyed her over the rim of the mug. Her hair hung loosely across her slender shoulders. She'd changed into sweatpants and a loose shirt. Somehow, she managed to look sexy even in comfy clothes. "How was the brewery?"

"It was great. Harold kept hitting on Amanda's coworker, who is at least ten years his senior."

He glanced at the clock on the wall. "It must not have been that great. It's still early."

She shifted her weight from one hip to the other and picked at her cuticles. "I left early. I wanted to come back and check on you. How's your ankle feeling?"

"It doesn't hurt too bad. Your mom gave me some strong pain meds."

"Good."

"I think it'll heal on its own as long as I don't put too much pressure on it. I might need to take a few days off work though." He frowned. The down time would kill him, especially if the arsonist started another fire. With no leads or clues, they couldn't predict where the arsonist would strike next.

Grace picked harder at her cuticles. "I should get to bed. Do you need anything else?"

He set his mug on the nightstand and glanced down

at her hands. "You're picking at your nails. You always used to do that in high school when you were nervous. Do you regret what happened today?"

She dropped her arms to her sides. "I don't regret kissing you. I wish I *did*, though."

He laughed. "That makes perfect sense."

"Being with you, kissing you, it feels right." Grace sighed. "But there are too many implications. Too many risks."

"You mean Liam and the possibility of me going back to the air force?"

"Yes ... No, that's not all."

Standing there with uncertainty plastered across her face, she looked so vulnerable. He had to comfort her. Keeping his wounded ankle on the pillow, he moved over in the bed and patted the open spot.

She glanced back at the door as if she was considering leaving the room, but then she walked toward the bed and slipped in next to him. Beneath the comforter, her leg brushed against his. "I can't do this again. You and me. It took me years to get over you. That's the main reason I didn't call you. If I'd heard your voice, I would've regretted my decision to leave." She paused. "I don't want to hurt either of us like that again."

He shifted to meet her gaze. The breakup had been just as hard on Grace. He wrapped his arms around her and pulled her against his chest, cupping the back of her head. More than anything, he wanted to kiss her again, but it would lead them into dangerous territory. He let go of her and leaned back against his pillows.

She lay on her side and rested her hand on his chest.

She could have come up with an excuse to leave by now, but she hadn't. Smiling, he closed his heavy eyelids, giving in to the effects of the pain medication. He drifted off into a deep sleep, enjoying the warmth of her body next to his.

In his sleep, dreams flitted from one memory to the next, finally traveling to his second deployment. He'd landed the helicopter to pick up a local girl who had been hit with rocket-propelled grenade fragments. As soon as his crew brought the little wounded girl inside the aircraft, the sound of gunfire erupted on all sides. Blood rushed to his face as he directed the aircraft off the landing zone to get them to safety.

One bullet pierced through the sheet metal between Seth and the flight engineer on the right side of the helicopter. It broke through Seth's Kevlar seat, hit his arm, sped across the cockpit, and went out through the main rotor blade.

The seat pan and bullet fragments flew across the small space and hit Caleb in the neck. His head jerked to the left, and he lost control of the helicopter.

"Caleb, are you all right?"

Nodding, he turned forward and gripped the console.

"Caleb." Gentle hands shook him to consciousness.

He blinked repeatedly, his blurry vision clearing to see Grace lying beside him.

Her forehead creased with worry. "You were shouting and shaking."

"I'm sorry." He sat up and leaned against the headboard.

"You don't have to be sorry." She moved to a sitting position beside him and rested her head on his shoulder. "It was a nightmare about the air force." She didn't need to ask.

Caleb wiped a bead of sweat trickling down his temple. "During my second deployment, I volunteered to go in place of one of my buddies, who had been shot a few days earlier. I didn't know the area very well, and on our first mission, we had a unique experience." He lightly stroked her forearm with his fingers.

She shivered and cuddled closer to him. "What happened?"

"We were picking up several patients who were in critical condition. After we picked up one of the patients, we were hit with small-arms fire. Seth was shot in the shoulder, and I lost control of the helicopter. My crew thought I was dead."

"Oh, Caleb. I hate that you're having nightmares. You have to relive that every night."

"I do have them almost every night, but I'm sure they'll stop after a while."

"And if they don't?"

He grimaced. "They're just dreams. I'm a big boy. I can handle it."

"Have you considered going to a counselor, someone who could—"

"Please don't." He put his pointer finger on her lips. "Don't try to fix me."

Grace looked at him for a moment before she sat up. She pushed his hand away and brought her lips to his.

Caleb stiffened. Last night, they'd agreed they wouldn't kiss again. The consequences were too high. But the flowery scent of her perfume intoxicated his senses, and the warmth of her lips traveled through his body.

He returned the kiss and brought his hand to the small of her back, pressing her closer. He wanted her just as badly as he had in high school, maybe more. If he could, he'd show her how a woman's body deserved to be treated. But he had to stop this before it went any further. Using all of his willpower, he gently pulled away.

A mixture of emotions flashed across her face. Her chest rose and fell as she looked away from him, her gaze resting on the sunshine pouring through his curtains. "I should get going." She slid out of bed and straightened her shirt.

"Okay." His voice sounded gruff.

Grace sent him a sweet smile before she disappeared down the hallway.

He fell back against his pillows and rubbed his temples. What were they doing? They shouldn't be together. It wasn't the right time for either of them.

Right? But now, he was questioning his decision to remain a bachelor. Because, dang it, he was drawn to her. She was the perfect combination of sweet, confident, honest, and beautiful. She encouraged him to open up in a way no one else could.

But he had to think about his future. If he reenlisted, he'd be the one leaving this time. He'd be the one breaking *her* heart. Could he carry that guilt with him for the rest of his life?

❧

GRACE TIPTOED DOWNSTAIRS to her apartment and rounded the corner to head toward her bedroom. The last floorboard creaked beneath her feet.

"Where were you?"

She ran her tongue over her teeth and turned around.

Mom sat at the kitchen table, dressed in a red blouse and white skirt. She toyed with a gold hoop earring.

"You're awfully dressed up this morning."

"We have church in an hour." Mom sat up straighter

and crossed her legs, showcasing her red high heels. "You didn't answer my question. Where were you?"

She squared her shoulders. "I was with Caleb."

Mom shook her head, causing her earrings to jingle.

"Before you judge me, nothing happened. We were talking, and we fell asleep. End of story."

Mom made a *tsk* noise. "Is it?"

"Is it, what?"

"Grace Elizabeth, it is *not* the end of the story. You have feelings for Caleb." Mom stood and tossed her uneaten toast in the garbage. "You should be thankful it was me sitting here and not Liam. What would you have told him?"

"I shouldn't have to explain myself to you."

"Next time you decide to have a sleepover in your boyfriend's room, you might need to figure out what to tell your son."

"Liam is at Davis's house." Grace bit the inside of her cheek. "You have no right to talk to me that way. I'm not a teenager anymore."

"Then stop acting like there won't be repercussions for your actions."

Letting out a frustrated growl, she strode to her bedroom. She was done with this conversation.

She closed her bedroom door and leaned back against it. Mom was wrong. She *had* thought about the consequences, she'd just ignored them. And for once, it felt good. Lying with Caleb, cuddling with him, letting him confide in her after his nightmare. She already ached to be back in his room with his arms wrapped around her.

She moved to her bed, fell back against the feather-stuffed comforter, and stared at the ceiling. *Oh, Caleb, what are we doing?*

Chapter 10

THE AIR-CONDITIONING KICKED on full force as the mayor walked around the dining room table and handed each committee member a packet of papers. "We've started remodeling essential places like the fire station, the doctor's office, police station, and post office." He stopped at the head of the table. "The development team has brought in a large construction crew to make this process as fast as possible. The faster they remodel, the sooner our town can start functioning again."

Caleb nodded. Finally, something he and Jennings could agree on.

"Knox has acquired most of the downtown business-es, except for the Canine Palace and Candy Galore." The mayor paused. "Unless, of course, you've changed your minds."

Caleb put his arm around the back of Dad's chair as an awkward silence filled the room.

Sandy clasped her hands together. A dark purple scar

colored the top of her right hand—a wound from the fire. "I've changed my mind. I have decided to sell. I was being stubborn and sentimental. It makes more sense to sell to Knox, especially considering the state of my store after the fire and the flood."

Jennings's eyes grew wide. "I'm happy to hear that."

Dad shook his head. "It might make sense for Sandy, but it doesn't for me."

Caleb's chest pinched with concern. What would happen if the mayor used eminent domain and took Dad to court for the property? More importantly, what would happen if Dad lost the business he loved?

"Let's move on to the next item of business." Jennings plopped down in a chair. He picked up the packet and turned to the third page. "This is a list of the original downtown stores that will be remodeled next."

Caleb scanned the list. Val's Diner, The Maple Valley Tribune, Dill's Grocery, The Joint, and Fern's Floral were all listed on the page.

"Wait a minute. Charger's Sporting Goods isn't on here." Charlie cracked his knuckles. "That store has been in my family for years. My sister-in-law owns it. She's a single mom. What is she supposed to do?"

"I'll address that store particularly in a minute. Knox had a strategic way of choosing. The twenty stores that made the most in sales in the last five years are the one's getting remodeled. The other stores will be replaced."

Dad rolled up his sleeves. "I'm curious. If I sold the Canine Palace to Knox, would it be on the list?"

The mayor opened a file folder and took out a piece of paper. After a moment, he said, "No, it wouldn't be." He turned his attention to Sandy. "Once you handle the legalities, Candy Galore will be on the list."

Sandy smiled. "That's wonderful."

Dad's eyebrows furrowed together. "You're telling me that because my store didn't make enough money, you won't remodel it?"

"Ray, this isn't an emotional decision." Jennings steepled his fingers beneath his double chin. "Every store owner will have other options. For instance, Charlie, your sister-in-law can sell sporting products to one of the other stores. And Ray, you can still make your specialty dog products and sell them to someone else. Maybe Dill's Grocery, perhaps?"

Dad mumbled something incoherent under his breath. "You don't get it. I didn't open the Canine Palace to get rich. I became a business owner because I like interacting with the people in this town. *I* want to be the one working."

Jennings gave Caleb a look—a plea for help.

Contemplating how to respond, he stood and walked to the coffee maker, then poured decaf in a mug. He leaned against the wall of cabinets to keep pressure off his sprained ankle, more out of habit than anything else.

After a week of icing it and keeping it elevated, his ankle didn't hurt anymore.

He took a drink of coffee and glanced at Jennings. "Isn't there some way my dad could keep his business without interfering with Knox Bennett's plans?"

"I can't play favorites. Knox has already decided that not all of the original stores can stay. It only makes sense to choose stores by comparing sales." Jennings turned to the next page of the packet. "As for the new stores, we have several options to choose from. We could add Walmart, Lowe's, Dick's Sporting Goods, Sam's … the list goes on and on, so take a look at it. Make a list of which ten stores you'd like to add and bring it to our next meeting."

Sandy glanced at Dad, whispering loudly. "So, we do get a choice after all." She rolled her eyes. "Which stores will steal the least amount of business from us?"

Jennings cleared his throat. "I also wanted to inform you that Knox has decided a bed-and-breakfast would be a better fit than a hotel."

"How did he come to that conclusion?" Caleb asked.

The mayor scratched the back of his neck. "Knox wants to rebuild Maple Valley as a tourist town. He said it would be a shame not to bring more people to our quaint little town next to the river."

Dad, Valerie, Dill, and Sandy all spoke at once, their angry voices rising above one another.

His grip tightened around the mug. "A tourist town?"

Jennings eased out of his chair and stood. He held his hands up, signaling for silence. "Listen. This is a good idea. It'll bring in added tax revenue and more sales for every store owner."

Caleb clenched his jaw. If Maple Valley became a tourist town, it would mean more traffic, more crowds, and less of a hometown atmosphere. "You should've told us Knox wanted to go in that direction."

"Mt. Point Development didn't come up with the idea until this week. We weren't trying to con any of you. I told you as soon as I knew."

"The whole atmosphere of downtown will change completely," Caleb said.

The mayor collected loose papers and the packet and stuck them inside his briefcase. "You say that like it's a bad thing."

Wasn't it? He took a drink of coffee, studying the committee members over the rim of his mug. Maybe he wasn't any different than Sandy. Too sentimental. Too stubborn to realize a change could be good. But could a tourist town really be better for Maple Valley's future?

❧

CALEB PUT HIS arm around Amanda's shoulders. "I can't

believe you're getting married soon, sis."

"I know. It's surreal." Amanda smiled. She glanced at the back porch.

Caleb followed her gaze to where Grace stood on a stool, holding a strand of white lights up against the pergola. Using her free hand, she positioned the stapler and pushed it into the wood. Her shirt lifted slightly, showcasing her flat torso.

His lips parted, and he had to force his gaze away.

"Here." Kendall unraveled more lights and lifted them up to Grace as Liam dashed by, almost crashing into the stool.

"Liam, please be careful," Grace said. "The bridal shower starts in an hour. I don't have time to fix the decorations if you knock them down."

"Sorry, Mom." Liam gripped the handle of a kite, running in a different direction and looking up at the sky. Instead of lifting, the kite dragged behind him in the grass.

Caleb chuckled. "I'm headed to Maple Valley to check out the new fire station and clean the trucks. I can take Liam with me so you can focus on the party."

Liam tucked the kite beneath his elbow and clasped his hands together, pleading. "Please, Mom?"

Grace twisted the strand of lights in her hand. "Are you sure, Caleb?"

"Yeah."

"Sweet!" Liam thrust his arm in the air.

Grace laughed. "I've never seen you so excited to clean before."

Liam rolled the string around his kite. "We're going to the fire station. It'll be a lot more fun than cleaning my room."

"Bring him back in one piece, Caleb."

"Of course." Winking, he walked past her and waved for Liam to follow him to the parking lot.

A half hour later, he stood side by side with Liam as they toured the remodeled fire station. The faded brick exterior was now a light shade of gray, and the two large garage doors glistened with a shiny red coat of paint.

In the kitchen, the construction crew had added stainless steel appliances and a brick backsplash; in the lounge, they'd added leather couches, a flat screen TV, and two ornate wooden tables filled with game boards that had been donated from a local church. A wall in the back of the station had been torn out, adding more space and privacy to the locker room, bathrooms, and bedroom.

At the end of the walk-through, a slow smile spread across Caleb's face.

Liam put his hands on his hips. "Why do you look so happy? Don't you work here all the time?"

He smiled. "Yeah, I do, but this is my first time seeing the station after it got remodeled. It looks amazing."

"Oh." Liam shrugged. "Can we go see the fire trucks now?"

"Sure." He walked into the garage, filled two buckets with soapy water, and set them beside the ladder truck.

Liam looked at the truck in awe. "Can we go for a ride?"

"Let's clean first. If you do a good job, I'll take you for a drive."

"Deal."

Caleb dunked his sponge in the soapy water, then scrubbed it over the driver's door. "Did you know that the Earth is the only known planet where fire can burn?"

Liam stopped scrubbing to look at him. "Uh-uh."

"Want to know something else interesting?"

"Yeah."

"No one knows who invented the fire hydrant because its patent was destroyed in a fire in 1836."

"What's a patent?" Liam asked.

"It's a document that says you're the creator of an invention."

"Oh." Liam looked at Caleb in awe. "How do you know all this stuff?"

"When I was in the air force, I read a lot."

"I like to read too." Liam squatted down and wiped the back tire. "Mostly graphic novels."

"Graphic novels?"

"You don't know what a graphic novel is? You *are* old."

Caleb choked back a laugh. "I'm the same age as your mom. We grew up together, remember?"

"I know. You've told me that before." Standing, Liam dropped his sponge in the bucket, a serious look spreading across his face. "Did you know my dad?"

Caleb turned to look at Liam. How was he supposed to respond to that? "I might have. Maple Valley is a small town, but your mom hasn't told me who your dad is."

"That's because she doesn't know," Liam said in a quiet tone. "I was hoping she'd fibbed to me about it, and she actually does know. Like maybe he's a secret agent or something. But I guess not."

"Oh."

"Terrible, huh? At least, that's what the kids at school say. When I told them, they started calling my mom names. Mean names I shouldn't repeat."

What? He squeezed all the water out of his sponge. "Listen to me. Your mom is one of the sweetest, most respectable people I've ever met. I can only guess what names she's been called, but those kids don't know what they're talking about."

"Really?" Liam bit his bottom lip. "I've looked up what those names mean and—"

"Trust me, buddy. Your mom is a good person."

Liam gave a shaky smile.

Suddenly, the fire alarms blared overhead. His pager went off, and the dispatcher's voice relayed the details. "Maple Valley fire, 1202 Ashmend Road, Val's Diner, structure fire, 1100 hours."

He cursed under his breath. Was it the arsonist again? If so, why would someone want to start a fire on new construction? Whatever the reason, Valerie would be devastated.

He gripped Liam's shoulders. "Go to the office and stay there. Can you do that for me, buddy?"

"Yeah."

Without waiting to see if Liam listened, Caleb ran to the locker room. He slipped into his boots and pulled up his pants and suspenders. Grabbing his hood, coat, mask, and helmet, he jogged back to the fire truck and hopped in the back seat.

On the way, the lieutenant assigned duties. It only took a few minutes to arrive at Val's Diner. Smoke rose above the building and crept out the windowpanes.

After following orders to unwind the hose, he peered closely at the building. One of the brand-new windows had been broken into. He squeezed the back of his neck. *Definitely, the arsonist.* "Chief, do you see that?" He pointed at the window as he put the rest of his gear on.

Jennings nodded. "Look for other signs of arson when you're in there."

"Got it."

Nash broke down the front door and led the others inside the smoky building.

Heat consumed the room, bleeding through Caleb's uniform. He followed the other firefighters into the kitchen as they blasted the source of the fire with a wide stream of water.

After thirty minutes, the fire was put out, and he scanned the room for clues. Dark smoke and steam clouded the kitchen, making it hard to see. He carefully maneuvered through the space. Nothing out of the ordinary.

He walked along the walls of the room, noticing the cabinet door beneath the sink was slightly ajar. He opened the door and swatted at the smoke. Coughing, he peered inside. A charred firework—similar to the one in Candy Galore and Fern's Floral—sat inside with the burnt remains of new pipes.

Anger simmered deep inside his core. What did the arsonist have against Maple Valley? What was the person trying to prove?

Gritting his teeth, he left the door open and strode outside with the rest of the crew. His eyes widened as Liam ran toward him.

"Wow! That was the coolest thing I've ever seen."

Taking deep breaths, Caleb removed his helmet and tried to keep his tone even. "What are you doing here?"

Liam froze for a moment. "Are you mad at me?"

"I told you to stay at the station."

"I hopped on the side of the truck and held on."

"You shouldn't have done that. You could've been hurt." He gestured with his hands as he spoke.

Liam dropped his chin. "I didn't think you'd mind. I just wanted to see you in action."

Caleb's throat thickened with emotion. He would never want anything bad to happen to Liam. He pulled the kid close and hugged him. "I'm not mad at you."

Liam noticeably swallowed.

Jennings waddled over and ruffled Liam's hair. "I've already talked to our friend about how dangerous his decision was." His gaze remained serious as he looked at Caleb. "I hope you'll make sure that never happens again."

"Yes, sir."

"Did you find anything inside?"

"Another firework. We've got to stop this criminal."

The mayor expelled a heavy sigh. "I agree."

Liam drew back, his eyebrows raising. "Did you say a *firework* started the fire?"

"Yeah. Why?" Caleb asked.

Fear flickered in Liam's eyes. "Nothing."

Shoot. Maybe he should've waited until Liam was out of earshot. The idea of a criminal starting fires probably scared him.

Caleb had to admit that even *he* was spooked. Whoever had started the fires in Candy Galore, Fern's Floral, and Val's Diner had gotten away with arson three times in a row. The person was gaining confidence, which meant he or she would probably start another fire.

So far, they were lucky that no one had been seriously hurt, but with a dangerous arsonist on the loose, their luck couldn't hold out forever.

GRACE BALANCED A notebook over one knee as she added *kitchen utensils* to the list of gifts Amanda had received from her bridal shower. She'd offered to make the list so the bride could write thank-you notes later. And also, to escape the limelight. Ethan had mentioned his family was nosy, but she hadn't expected his mom and sisters to cast their attention on *her*. As the only single woman at the party, his sisters found it necessary to tell her all about their single cousins who would be at the wedding. His sisters meant well, but she wasn't a charity case. She was single. What was so bad about that?

You're lonely. The answer came all too quickly. Ignoring the voice in her head, she looked at the soon-to-be bride.

Amanda sat beneath the pergola wearing a sleeveless white dress. Curly blond strands fell in waves across her tan shoulders as she unwrapped a large Crock-Pot and a

Greek recipe cookbook. Smiling, she looked at Ethan's aunt. "Are you trying to give me a hint?"

His aunt shook her head, then laughed and nodded. "I'll come over and teach you a few of my own too."

"That would be wonderful." Amanda lowered the Crock-Pot to the porch and picked up the last gift—a tall silver bag full of bathroom accessories.

Grace wrote quickly as her friend lifted each item out of the bag.

Behind her, two nurses from Amanda's birth center spoke excitedly about the bride and groom. How they were perfect together. How they would probably get pregnant right away. How they would have at least three kids.

An unexpected ache squeezed inside her chest. What was wrong with her? She was happy for Amanda.

Okay, maybe she was *a little* jealous. Amanda was so open to love. When she'd met Ethan, she had just broken up with her boyfriend of four years. A boyfriend who she wanted to marry. But Amanda opened her heart to Ethan and now they were starting their new life together.

Grace glanced down at her ring-less hand. If she had put herself out there, she could've fallen in love by now. She could've been married.

But she'd made excuses instead.

She was too cautious. Too much of a planner. Years

ago, her plan included marrying Caleb. She'd dreamed of being one of those girls who dated the same boy all throughout her teens and married her high school sweetheart.

Caleb was the ultimate plan that fell through.

She didn't like making new plans. That had to be why she kept thinking of him at night before she went to sleep, and why he was the first person she pictured when she woke up.

Amanda clasped her hands together. "Thank you for the gifts, everyone. I'm looking forward to spending the week with all of you before I become Mrs. Contos."

As soon as Amanda rose from her seat, the guests mingled with people from other tables.

Grace set the notebook on Amanda's chair as Caleb's truck pulled into the parking lot. Liam got out and skipped toward her with Caleb trailing behind him.

"Hey, kiddo." She wrapped her arms around his thin frame. "Did you guys have fun?"

Liam squirmed out of her embrace. A goofy grin stretched from ear to ear. "It was the best day ever."

"Wow, the best day ever?" She raised her eyebrows.

"Yeah. I got to ride in the fire truck and watch Caleb put out a real fire."

What? Heat rose up the back of her neck. She sent Caleb a questioning look.

He rocked back on his heels. "About that. I told

Liam to stay at the station when we got the call, but he hopped onto the truck anyway. I didn't see him until we'd finished putting out the fire."

She folded her arms across her chest. "Liam, we aren't done talking about this. But right now, I need to talk to Caleb alone."

Her son's smile faltered. "Don't get mad at him."

"Please go," she said quietly.

As soon her son trudged inside the bed-and-breakfast, she glared at Caleb. "Why didn't you check to make sure he'd listened to you?"

"I didn't have time. And once we got the call, all I could think about was getting to the fire."

She let out a frustrated breath. "Look, I get that you were focused on your job, but my son was with you. He was *your* responsibility when you offered to take him." She put her hands on the back of her head. "What if something bad had happened to him? What if—"

"Yeah, something bad could've happened, but it didn't." Caleb stepped closer to her and put his hands on her hips. "Liam's fine. And you heard him, it was the *best day ever*."

She shook her head and pushed his hands away. "You're not a parent. You don't understand."

"Why are you so mad at me?"

"I'm frustrated because I trusted you with my son." She rubbed her temples. "You don't know anything about taking care of kids. I never should've let Liam go with you."

A mixture of hurt and anger flashed across Caleb's face. "I would never let anything bad happen to him."

She slid her tongue along the front of her teeth. She had no doubt that he meant what he said, but it didn't change the fact that Liam could've gotten hurt.

"I need to tell you something."

"There's more?"

"Liam told the other kids at school that you don't know who his father is." Caleb spoke slowly as if it pained him to tell her. "They've been making fun of him and calling you names."

His words felt like a sucker punch to her gut, and she had to work at breathing. Kids were making fun of Liam? Was that why he'd had a hard time making friends this year?

Caleb put his hand under her chin, lifting it. "I already talked to Liam. I'm sure there's more to say, but he was smiling after our conversation."

Her eyebrows rose. "Really?"

"Yeah."

"I wish he would've told me."

"If I had to guess, he was scared, and he didn't want to make you feel bad."

"That's probably true." She bit her bottom lip. Caleb's concern, coming on the heels of her fears about the fire, had turned her insides into an emotional blender.

Liam and Caleb had developed a close bond. On one hand, it was sweet. Caleb liked spending time with her son. But that was the problem. Maybe they'd spent too much time together. How would Liam cope if Caleb reenlisted and never came back? Would her son be heartbroken, like she had been when her father left?

On the day her father moved out, she'd woken up to find her mom crying. Her father left a note saying he'd met someone else, and he wasn't coming back. He left a check, as if money could make up for his absence.

Of course, Caleb had much better reasons for leaving. She respected his sense of duty to serve and protect the country.

But had he considered how his absence would affect Liam? How it would affect her?

The smart thing to do would be to tell him that she couldn't see him anymore. Not until he'd made a decision about the air force. It wasn't fair to Liam. It wasn't fair to her. "It was fun while it lasted," wasn't that how the saying went? They could think fondly of the last four months with no hard feelings and move on with their lives.

The plan made sense. But could she go through with it?

Chapter 11

G RACE WALKED FROM one end of the yard to the other, examining the wedding decorations. On one side, a hundred and one chairs sat facing a wooden trellis with pink and yellow peonies attached to the rectangular frame. A large open tent was set up on the other side of the yard with white lights draped across the ceiling and a crystal chandelier hanging from the center. Circular tables were spread out beneath the tent, showcasing cedar-wood centerpieces with rustic lanterns, candles, and flowers.

Satisfied, she put her hands on her hips. Tomorrow night, with the white lights shining and the moon casting a dim glow over the yard, it would be the perfect setting for her best friend's wedding.

It didn't seem possible that the weekend was already here. Four months of planning, and it all came down to tomorrow. Why wasn't she more stressed? Or concerned about something going wrong? Or worried about messing up a Greek tradition?

Probably because her worries revolved around *after* the wedding. Like how she planned to have a long talk with Liam before she called the school counselor. She had to make sure someone would watch out for him when school started in the fall. He would probably be upset with her for mentioning it to the counselor, but the school had to be aware of the bullying to stop it from happening again.

And that wasn't all. She had to talk to Caleb about the future. Would he decide to stay? If not, what would happen between them? Would he move back to Maple Valley with the rest of the guests or would he reenlist?

A lump formed in her throat.

Mom opened the back door and stepped outside. Boisterous laughter floated through the yard.

Grace almost smiled. The rest of Ethan's relatives had arrived from Greece this morning, checking in to Cedar Crest and replacing some of the Maple Valley families who had recently left. In a matter of hours, Ethan's relatives had taken over the mansion, filling it with warmth and laughter.

Mom walked across the yard, wearing white dress pants and a red silky blouse. "What are you still doing out here? The rehearsal dinner starts in an hour."

"I know."

The crow's-feet around Mom's eyes grew deeper. "Is something wrong?"

She wrapped her arm around Mom's waist. "I wish Cedar Crest would stay this way forever. When we decided to open a bed-and-breakfast, this is what I imagined. A full house. Families playing board games in the dining room, people lounging by the fireplace, or friends sitting on the porch enjoying warm summer nights."

"I did too. The revenue we earned from Maple Valley guests and from Amanda's wedding will keep us open for the next few months. But after that ..." Mom let the sentence trail off as she looked at the old mansion with a faraway look in her eyes.

"I created new ads, and I'm planning to post them on social media next week. Hopefully, it'll make a difference."

"What if it doesn't?"

She'd asked herself the same question. Should she give up and go back to being a social worker? It didn't feel right but owning a failing business wasn't an option. Not when she had Liam to consider. Her current income would not support extracurricular activities, sports, or a college education.

She blew out a breath. "Honestly, I don't know what we should do. For now, let's focus on the wedding. Once it's over, we'll come up with a plan."

"You're right. One step at a time." Mom scanned the decorated yard. "It looks amazing."

"I'm really happy with how it turned out. I hope Amanda loves it. She's coming over to look at it before the rehearsal dinner."

"Then, you should go inside and take a shower. You stink." Mom pinched her nose before breaking into a smile.

Grace nudged her in the ribs and stepped out of their embrace. "Okay, okay. I'm going." With every step toward Cedar Crest, the voices inside grew louder.

A heavy weight pressed against her chest. She had no idea how to save her bed-and-breakfast, and she was just as uncertain when it came to Caleb. What was she supposed to do?

❦

CALEB REACHED FOR the last piece of baklava on his plate and enjoyed the sweet, flaky pastry as it filled his mouth. Swallowing, he leaned back in his chair and rubbed his stomach. He'd have to visit this cozy Greek restaurant again soon. "I'm stuffed."

Grace dropped her fork on her half-empty plate and folded her napkin into a small square. Was she still mad about the fire, or was she upset about the teasing Liam had endured?

Probably both.

He hadn't meant for Liam to come with him; she

had to understand that. And he'd only told her about the name-calling because if he were a parent, he would want to know if someone was making fun of his kid. It seemed like the right thing to do, but her sober expression claimed otherwise. He sighed. This weekend was supposed to be enjoyable.

Across the table, Amanda reached for Grace's hand. "Thank you for finding this place. It's a gem."

Ethan licked his lips. "Not many restaurants around here can make authentic Greek food like this. We'll have to come here more often. It reminds me of home."

Home. Caleb frowned. Where was home? Was it anywhere the air force stationed him? Was it in Maple Valley? With white-trimmed windows on the storefronts, new siding in shades of gray and slate blue, and paved streets with perfectly straight streetlamps, Maple Valley looked like a posterboard tourist town. It was barely recognizable.

Standing, Ethan tapped his fork against a glass of champagne. "Could I have everyone's attention?" He waited until the crowded table grew quiet. "On behalf of Amanda and myself, thank you for coming. We appreciate the time you're taking out of your busy lives to celebrate with us."

Amanda rose from her chair and put her hand over her chest. "Our wedding wouldn't be the same without you. We hope you enjoy every moment."

"To end the evening, I have a surprise for my bride-to-be." Ethan grinned as Amanda looked at him, her eyes widening. "I need everyone to follow me outside."

Following Ethan to the back porch, Caleb walked side by side with Liam and Grace. "What's going on?"

Grace shrugged. "I have no idea." She turned her back on him and put her arm around Liam's shoulders as she looked up at the star-filled sky. "Do you see Orion's belt?"

Liam nodded. "Yeah. It's really bright."

Caleb walked a few feet ahead and rested his elbows on the porch railing. Yup. She was still mad at him.

A loud boom exploded in the sky, followed by a burst of red—a firework in the shape of a big red heart.

Many of their family members oohed and aahed, clapping as the heart faded into the darkness.

Caleb gripped the railing as more fireworks shot off. His whole body tensed. It sounded like the mortars that enemies would shoot at their base. Like the time he'd been working on the helicopter and mortars flew past him, inches away from his shoulder. He ducked down and fled to safety, but he was so shaken up he spent several hours talking to a chaplain and smoking cigars.

Now, he fought the urge to flee. He'd heard from other pilots that the first Fourth of July was the hardest. But he hadn't been prepared for fireworks tonight. He squeezed his eyes shut and took several deep breaths. *It's not mortars. It's just fireworks.*

Despite his efforts to calm down, his heart raced faster. He opened his eyes, but his vision blurred. Acid burned the back of his throat as waves of nausea rolled through his stomach.

Grace appeared at his side, putting her hand on his lower back. "Let's go." She guided him off the porch.

In the shadows of the restaurant, he bent over and emptied his stomach until there was nothing left.

She stood behind him, rubbing his back. "It's okay. You're safe."

He wiped his mouth with the back of his hand. "Can you take me back to Cedar Crest?"

"Of course. My mom can take Liam home." Grace took his keys, hopped inside, and started his truck. "I just had an idea. Would it be all right if we go somewhere else?"

"Sure."

After sending a quick text to her mom, she turned off the radio and headed into town.

The tension in his neck loosened. He opened the passenger's side window and rested his head against the seat. The warm summer air rushed over his face. How embarrassing. He'd never had an incident in public where his PTSD had affected him like that.

His phone vibrated in his pocket. Caleb glanced at the screen, reading a text from Ethan. *Sorry about the fireworks. I wasn't thinking. Hope you're all right.*

Caleb frowned. *I am now. Thanks for checking in.*

How many friends and family members had seen him lose it? At least Grace had noticed quickly before he could ruin the end of the rehearsal dinner. "Thank you for getting me out of there. Especially when you're still upset with me."

"I'm not mad at you."

"You barely talked to me during dinner, and you walked away from me when we were on the porch."

"I wasn't doing it on purpose. I've been in my head a lot." She tapped her index finger on the steering wheel. "The truth is it bothers me that Liam talked to you instead of me. I thought he knew he could tell me anything."

"I'm sure he knows that. But Liam and I have grown close over the last few months."

"That's the other problem."

His eyebrows furrowed together. "I don't understand."

"I'm worried that you've grown too close. Liam will be devastated if you leave and go back to the air force." She stared straight ahead, lowering her voice as if talking to herself. "I don't want Liam to feel abandoned."

"That's the last thing I'd ever want to do."

She glanced in his direction. "If you do decide to reenlist, would you do me a favor?"

"Sure. What is it?"

"Talk to Liam. Tell him why you're leaving so he doesn't blame himself, like I did when my dad left."

"Of course." *So that was what had been bothering her.* It made sense, considering how her dad had abandoned her and her mom.

A sour taste filled Caleb's mouth. He hadn't thought of Liam's feelings. He hadn't thought of his own either. He would miss building Lego towns with Liam. He would miss their discussions about firefighting or seeing the look of admiration Liam gave him when he spoke about the air force.

He scrubbed a hand over his clean-shaven face. For the first time since he'd reconnected with Grace, he understood the complexity of her decisions. She couldn't just think about herself. She had to weigh the pros and cons of choices for Liam as well.

What would that type of responsibility feel like? To raise and protect a life so deeply connected to his own?

"We're here." Grace pulled into the parking lot of Rex Mathes Elementary School. She pulled a thin white sweater out of her purse and slid it on over her pink flowery dress. "Come with me." She got out of the truck, her heels clicking against the pavement.

He peered out the open window. Outside lights on the school illuminated the playground. What were they doing here? He wanted to ask her, but she'd already walked away, heading toward the swing set.

He followed her to the playground and sat down in one of the swings. "Why are we here?"

"When Liam was a toddler, I took him to the playground for the first time. I was so busy thinking about how much fun he'd have swinging and going down slides that I didn't consider how it would affect me." As she spoke, she took off her heels and set them on the ground. "Even though I'd healed in many ways, I couldn't walk any farther than the sandbox at the edge of the park. I knew it was safe, but my body reacted differently as if the man who'd attacked me was standing on the jungle gym set, watching me."

"How long did it take before you could go back without getting triggered?"

"A few times." Grace shifted in the swing, turning toward him slightly. "I learned how to cope by reminding myself that I was safe. I repeated it over and over again."

He met her gaze with a newfound appreciation. Although Grace had experienced a completely different trauma than him, she knew what he was going through. She understood the turmoil of PTSD, and she'd learned how to cope with it. "I'll have to try that next time."

"It doesn't have to control you."

"That's true." He kicked his feet forward and backward, propelling the swing into motion. Somehow,

Grace had a way of easing his distress by sharing in it. "Remember how you told me to go see a counselor?"

"Yeah."

"Well, I'm beginning to think you're right."

Her gaze followed him as he swung back and forth. "I'm glad. I think it'll really help."

Caleb stuck his shoes on the ground, skidding to a stop. He hopped off the swing.

"What are you doing?"

Without answering her question, he stood behind her and pushed.

She gave him a look of disbelief. "Caleb Meyers, we are not children anymore."

"It feels kinda liberating." He pushed her again. "And you're the one who wanted to come to the playground."

"For metaphorical purposes." She laughed, a soft pleasant sound that wrapped around his heart.

How did their conversation go from serious to fun in a matter of minutes? It seemed to happen a lot lately. Part of it was the comfortability level they had after years of growing up together. Part of it was the experiences they'd had while they were apart. And part of it—a big part of it—was the connection they shared now.

He couldn't deny it. They were good together.

A sharp pulse of alarm coursed through him. He was falling for her. *Again.*

Chapter 12

GRACE PULLED A small tissue out of her pink and yellow bouquet and dabbed it at the corners of her eyes. She couldn't help it. Amanda looked radiant in her sleek, silk wedding dress. A traditional Greek crown made with flowers, foliage, and ribbon wrapped around her head, and her big blond curls cascaded down her back.

She smiled. This was it. The moment her best friend had dreamed about since they were little girls.

So far, the day had been perfect, or close to it. One small hiccup. When Amanda was getting dressed, she couldn't find her shoes. They weren't in her bridal bag. After an hour of panicking, Ethan's mom brought them to Amanda. She'd taken the shoes in order to write all the single women's names on the bottom of the soles. Apparently, it was a tradition in their family, and the names that wore off by the end of the reception were the women who would soon get married. When Ethan's mom explained her reasoning to Amanda, she'd looked pointedly at Grace.

Besides that incident, everything had gone according to plan. Hopefully, the rest of the day would go just as smoothly.

Grace snuck a peek at Caleb. He wore a navy tux that fit snugly over his broad shoulders, and his short hair was styled. He stared at his sister, a mixture of awe and curiosity plastered across his handsome face.

She licked her lips. What was he thinking?

He must've felt her gaze because he turned to look at her.

Her chest rose and fell. Would he ever reconsider settling down and getting married? Was she silly for questioning it? She resisted the urge to shake her head. Today was about Amanda and Ethan. She needed to get Caleb off her mind.

❧

AT THE RECEPTION, Caleb clapped with the other wedding guests as Amanda and Ethan walked toward the dessert table. Amanda's rosy cheeks were flushed, and her smile grew wider with each passing hour. He'd never seen his sister so happy.

She picked up a cupcake and stuck her finger in the frosting, then smeared the cream all over her husband's face. Ethan laughed and pulled Amanda close, kissing her with his frosting-covered lips.

Amanda giggled. "Best kiss ever." She picked up a napkin and wiped her face. "That frosting is delicious. Now, I want the rest." She took a bite of the Red Velvet cupcake.

Caleb grinned, waiting for her reaction. *Three, two, one …*

Swallowing, she turned and searched the nearby crowd until she met his gaze. "Is this Mom's recipe?"

He nodded.

"Oh, Caleb." Moisture built in her eyes. "Did you request it when you did the cake tasting?"

"Yup."

She walked toward him and wrapped her arms around his neck. "This means so much to me."

"I wanted Mom to be a part of this day just as much as you did."

Dad stepped between them and reached for their hands. He squeezed them three times—his way of saying "I love you."

"I wish Mom was here," Amanda said.

"Me too, Minnow. She would've enjoyed every second of today."

"Yes, she would have." Amanda grinned. "Ethan and I need to make the rounds and say hello to everyone. I'll catch up with you two later." She kissed Caleb's cheek. "Thanks again."

As she walked away, Dad took off his tuxedo jacket and folded it over one arm. "You're a good brother. Your mom would've been pleased. She loved that recipe."

"It was the least I could do."

"Speaking of love." Dad's bushy eyebrows rose and fell. "What's going on between you and Grace? You've barely taken your eyes off her all day."

He loosened the knot in his tie. "You're exaggerating." But even as he spoke, he glanced over at her. Heat pooled low in his stomach.

She stood by the dance floor, talking with her mom as they watched Ethan's relatives hold hands and dance in a circle. She looked gorgeous in a pink dress that cut across one shoulder, wrapped around her flat torso, and cut off just above her knees. Her hair was swept into a bun with little ringlets framing her face. She wore more makeup than normal, including eyeliner, rose-colored eye shadow, and a similar lipstick shade to match.

Dad cleared his throat. "I may be old, but I'm not crazy. I know what I see."

"Okay, Casanova." Caleb forced his gaze away from Grace to look at his dad. "What about you and Sandy? What's going on with you two?"

"She asked me to move in permanently."

"Wow. What did you tell her?"

"I'm gonna do it." Dad smiled, but a sober expression crossed his features. "I've been meaning to tell you something else … I sold the Canine Palace to Mt. Point Development."

Caleb's mouth hung open. "You're kidding."

Dad chuckled. "No, I'm not."

"Why would you give it up, Dad? What was the point of fighting for it?"

"There wasn't a point. That's what I came to realize."

"How can you say that?"

"I loved running the Canine Palace. It gave me a fresh start. It brought Amanda and I closer when she helped me open the business. And co-owning it with someone like Charlie, who has a lot more business sense than I do, has helped me learn a great deal." Dad took off his glasses and cleaned them with a small handkerchief from his pocket. "But I'm ready to retire. I need to stop fighting for a place I'm going to let go of soon."

"What about Charlie? I thought he was planning to take over when you retired."

"He was, but he recently decided to co-own Dick's Sporting Goods with his sister-in-law, Hannah."

"Oh."

"Plus, without the Canine Palace, Candy Galore can have a larger space. Sandy plans to make a little room in her store for my dog treats. She wants to call them Doggy Delicacies."

Caleb grinned. "Ah, so this is about Sandy."

"My feelings for her have nothing to do with this

decision."

"Sure, sure." He laughed. "If it all works out, maybe she'll let you work there full time."

"I have no such plans. I'm going to enjoy retirement to its fullest: take long naps, play poker with my buddies, go fishing with Ethan." Dad's eyes sparkled. "And play with my future grandchildren."

"Sounds like you have it all planned out."

"Nope. That's the best part. I don't." Dad rocked back on his heels. "You don't have to have everything figured out. Just the next step."

The next step. What was *his* next step? Stay and build a life in Maple Valley or reenlist to serve his country?

"Stop thinking so hard. Your eyebrows are practically pinched together in a unibrow. Not a very flattering look for you, son."

He shook his head. "Do you hear what comes out of your mouth sometimes?"

"I get that you're confused about your future. Just remember, your purpose can change even when you don't. No matter what you decide, you're a protector. When you and your sister were kids, you always tried to protect her from mean kids on the playground, from almost getting tangled in my fishing line ..." Dad paused for a moment before continuing. "When you were in the air force, you protected our country. And since you've been home, you've been protecting me."

What is the old man's point?

"Your next step depends on what you want to protect in the future." Dad squeezed Caleb's shoulder. "Let me ask you an important question. What's worth fighting for now? Is it your country? Or is it Grace and Liam?"

He stiffened.

"When you have the answer, that's when you'll know what to do."

"How did you get so wise?"

Dad's eyes crinkled. "I've been wise for many years. You're just starting to see it."

Caleb nodded. Despite Dad's lighthearted tone, the depth of the conversation sank into his core. He had a lot to think about.

"Enough talking. I want a cupcake." Dad patted his midsection before walking toward the dessert table.

Valerie sauntered over to him, wearing a sleek black dress and high heels. "Hey, stranger. Now that I'm back in Maple Valley, I miss seeing you at the bed-and-breakfast every day." She took a sip of wine. "It's so quiet in my house. Maybe you could come over, and I'll cook you breakfast sometime."

He squeezed the back of his neck. "I'm not sure when I'll be back in Maple Valley."

"Why not? Isn't your old apartment building open to renters again?"

"Yeah, it is." He glanced at Grace as her mom walked

off to sit at one of the tables. Now was his chance to ask her to dance. He gently touched Valerie's elbow. "Could we catch up later?"

"Oh. Um, sure." She tucked a dark strand of hair behind her ear.

He strode across the yard and leaned in close to Grace's ear to whisper, "You look beautiful."

She eyed him up and down. "You look pretty spiffy yourself."

"Want to dance?" He held out his hand as the band played "Truly, Madly, Deeply."

She glanced at Liam and her mom sitting at a table. Her mom was looking right at them with a mixture of intrigue and worry.

He moved slightly, blocking her mom from view. "I'm not taking no for an answer." He took her hand and pulled her out onto the dance floor.

She pretended to look offended but fell easily into step with him and wrapped her arms around his neck. Her fingers ran through his hair, sending tingles down his spine.

He put his hand on the small of her back and pulled her closer. The sweet scent of her flowery perfume enveloped his senses. Heat spread from his head to his toes, igniting a deep longing. In this moment, nothing else mattered. Not the past, not the future, just now. Because in this moment, she fit into his arms perfectly.

In this moment, she was his girl.

Was that what he wanted?

Her, yes. Staying here, being a fireman for the rest of his life, was another matter.

He stopped dancing and lifted her chin so he could meet her gaze. Even if he hadn't decided what to do, he had to tell her how he felt. "Grace …"

"Yes?" she asked breathlessly.

"I'm falling in love with you."

Grace noticeably swallowed. She opened her mouth, then closed it.

"You don't have to say anything. I wanted to be honest with you."

Her eyes filled with a flicker of hope. "Does this mean you're staying?"

"I'm not sure."

She ran her tongue along the front of her teeth and dropped her hands to her sides. "Of course you're not."

"Can't I tell you how I feel without having the rest of my life figured out?" The moment he said it, her face fell. He hadn't meant to sound so harsh.

"You're being selfish." She stepped back.

Selfish? He shook his head. This was not the reaction he'd been hoping for. "I think you're just looking for an excuse for us not to work out." He stormed off without waiting for her response.

⊰⊱

FINDING AN EMPTY table beneath the tent, Grace sat down and rested her achy feet on a nearby chair. After the sun disappeared below the horizon, many people had left, including Ray, Sandy, Kendall, and her husband. But the dance floor was still full, mostly with Ethan's family, plus Caleb.

After their dance, he'd disappeared for an hour, then spent the rest of the night dancing with Valerie.

Grace chewed on the inside of her cheek. Was he trying to make her jealous? If so, it was definitely working.

Caleb twirled Valerie around, laughing as she lost her balance and he caught her in his arms.

Ugh. She couldn't watch anymore. She moved to a different chair at the table, keeping her back to the dance floor.

"I brought you a cup of coffee." Mom slipped into a chair next to Grace and handed her the warm mug.

"Thanks." She cupped her hands around the mug and drummed her fingers along the porcelain.

Mom peered at her, her eyes filled with compassion and understanding. "I owe you an apology."

"For what?"

"I was wrong about you and Caleb." Mom pushed her shoulders back and crossed her legs. "The chemistry between you is undeniable. I think you should give him a chance."

She took a sip of coffee. "Why are you telling me this now?"

Mom expelled a deep breath. "After your dad left us, I was blindsided and heartbroken. And truth be told, I never got over it."

"I had no idea." Grace gave her a sad smile. "You've always seemed so strong and independent."

"I didn't want you to worry about me." Mom twisted one of the rings on her finger. "I discouraged you from being with Caleb because I wanted to protect you. I didn't want you to get hurt like I'd been." She reached across the table and put her hand over Grace's. "You deserve to be happy. But that means you have to take a risk. You have to give someone your heart. If that someone is Caleb, you should go for it."

Her shoulders lowered. "I think it's too late."

Mom glanced in the direction of the dance floor. "Oh, please. He might be dancing with Valerie, but I've seen him look over at you several times."

Heat crept into her cheeks. "Oh."

"It's getting late." Mom stood. "I'll take Liam to bed. If you don't come back to the apartment tonight, I'll cover for you."

She gave a shaky laugh. "I'll keep that in mind." She turned and looked over her shoulder.

Caleb and Valerie were no longer on the dance floor.

Grace scanned the thinning crowd but didn't see them. She frowned. She could've danced with him all night, enjoying his company while she soaked up his words. He was falling in love with her. And all she'd done was judge him and accuse him of being selfish.

What was wrong with her? She should apologize. She left the reception and headed inside to his room.

Her heart pounded hard against her chest. Even if Caleb left to reenlist, she had to tell him how she really felt. She stopped outside his door and lifted her hand to knock.

A female voice carried through the wall. *Valerie.*

Grace stared at the door. A sour taste filled her mouth. Disgust rolled through her stomach. How could Caleb say he was falling in love with her, then sleep with someone else the same night?

She turned on her heels and strode toward the basement. And how could she have been so stupid? Falling for someone who had no plan in life. Someone who made rash, emotional decisions.

This was for the better. Before Liam got his hopes up. Before she had her heart broken.

A tear slipped down her cheek. Who was she kidding? It was already too late. In hindsight, she should have known better. She should have guarded her heart from the only man she'd ever loved.

Chapter 13

THE BELL DOWNSTAIRS chimed again, capturing Grace's attention. Guests from the wedding had been checking out all morning.

She walked into the foyer and stopped mid-step.

Valerie and Caleb stood in the open doorway. Valerie walked out the door and blew Caleb a kiss. "Thanks for everything last night."

Grace's body tensed. She spun around before Caleb saw her and beelined for the staircase.

"Grace, I need to check out."

So much for not noticing her. *Wait.* He was leaving? She forced her feet to move toward the front desk. "You've already paid, so you just need to sign out." She pointed to the guestbook, barely able to look at him.

Caleb signed his name and the date. He picked up his duffle bag and slung the strap over his broad chest. "Well ..."

Ugh. That's all he has to say? She deserved more than that. She had to ask, or it would drive her crazy. "Are you going back to Maple Valley?"

"Yeah. I'm moving into my old apartment building. I'm signing a six-month lease this afternoon."

She lifted her gaze. "Why only six months?"

"I'm reenlisting after that."

No, no, no. Would he change his mind if she told him how she felt? How she spent every free moment thinking about him? How she craved his kisses? His touch?

She bit her bottom lip. She couldn't tell him any of that. Not after the way he'd reacted last night, storming off, then taking Valerie back to his room. Her heart ached just thinking about it.

He adjusted the strap over his shoulder. "I'll see you around."

As he walked away, her knees wobbled. She dropped her forehead to the desk and squeezed her eyes shut. Moisture built behind her eyelids.

She missed him already.

An hour later, she swept the floor in Caleb's empty room. Being in here, with the scent of his woodsy cologne drifting up from the bedsheets, it was hard to think straight. Had she made a mistake? Should she have at least asked him what happened with Valerie?

Her temples throbbed with indecision. Ignoring the oncoming headache, she leaned over and stuck the sweeper under the bed. It hit a lightweight object. She bent down on her knees and pulled out an envelope.

She turned it over, her eyebrows raising. The envelope was addressed to her at the house she'd grown up in. Had Caleb written this to her? She quickly dismissed the thought. This wasn't his handwriting. Who had written it, then?

She opened the flap and unfolded the lined notebook paper. Her eyes traveled down to the letter, reading the heavy, slanted script.

Dear Grace,

There is no excuse for what happened on the playground. I'm sorry for the pain I caused you. Not a day goes by when I don't think about what happened that night. I regret it. I wanted to apologize in person, but I can't. You're always with Caleb, and it would kill him if he knew. Actually, I think Caleb would kill me. But if you tell him, I'd understand.

I never should've tried to come between you two. It's just that I love you. I've loved you ever since I moved in next door to you. It's not an excuse, but I wanted you to know.

Seth

Every sentence caused bile to burn in the back of her throat. When she finished the letter, she let it drop to the wooden floorboards. Shock radiated through her body.

Seth had raped her? Her friend? And he'd tried to justify it by telling her that he'd loved her.

That wasn't love. He'd been obsessed and possessive. If he'd truly loved her, he would've given her a choice.

She ran into the attached bathroom, leaned over the toilet, and began dry-heaving. She stared at the toilet through blurry eyes. Reading his letter had brought back those memories of the playground, of the night she'd lost her innocence.

She sank to the bathroom floor, burying her head in her hands. Anger and bitterness crept into her heart. Seth had broken her. He'd made her feel weak and unworthy.

Big wet tears streamed down her cheeks. She pulled her knees to her chest and rocked back and forth as sobs shook her body.

Eventually, her sobs ebbed. Getting upset didn't change things. She'd cried far too many tears over what Seth had done to her. And yet, grief didn't have a timeline. It came and went, slithering into her heart with a single memory.

But now, her sense of betrayal cut even deeper. Caleb must have read this letter too. The flap on the envelop had a broken piece of tape on it. How long had he known? Had the letter been inside Seth's box?

It didn't matter. Caleb had no right to keep this letter a secret.

AT THE FIRE station, Caleb set his elbows on the table as he stacked and restacked a deck of cards. A group of firefighters sat on the other side of the table, playing a game of poker. They'd asked him to join in, but he'd declined.

Ever since his conversation with Grace at the reception desk, loneliness had carved a hole inside his chest. She didn't want to give him a chance. After their dance, he'd gone back to his room and resisted the urge to convince her otherwise.

Instead, he left his room and asked Valerie to dance. He knew she would say yes. What he hadn't accounted for was how many drinks she'd consumed before he asked, and how he would have to take care of her.

He barely slept last night. He tossed and turned, contemplating Dad's advice about the future. Even if he wanted to stick around and pursue a relationship with Grace, she'd made her intentions clear.

Just because he was in love with her didn't mean everything else would fall into place. The more he thought about it, the more he realized her response was meant to be. It was a sign that he was supposed to return to the air force, where he belonged.

The secretary's voice came over the loudspeaker. "Meyers, there's someone here to see you."

He stood from the table. Who was here? He rounded the corner and caught sight of Grace. His heart skipped a beat. Why was she here? Had she changed her mind?

When she saw him, her full lips turned downward, and she folded her arms across her chest. "We need to talk. Can we go outside?"

"Uh, sure." He followed her out to the parking lot. *Uh-oh.* Whatever she wanted to say, it wasn't good. "Is this about Valerie?"

She glared at him. "No. But I heard that you took her back to your room."

Heat crept up the back of his neck. He should've explained what happened earlier. But this morning, he'd been too preoccupied to think about it. Telling Grace that he planned to reenlist had caused a sharp knife-like pain to twist inside his gut. "Listen, nothing happened between Valerie and me."

"You don't have to explain."

"I don't want you to have the wrong idea." He stepped closer and reached out to touch her, but she held up her hand to stop him. "Valerie had too much to drink, and I didn't want her to drive home. I let her sleep in my bed while I slept on the floor."

"Oh."

He held her gaze with open eyes, hoping she could sense the truth.

Finally, she blew out a breath and pulled an envelope

out of her purse. "I didn't come here to talk about Valerie. I came here to talk about this. You forgot it under your bed."

"What is it?"

Anger flashed in her eyes. "I thought it was possible you were telling the truth about Valerie, but if you're pretending not to know about the letter, then maybe you're lying about last night too."

"I have no idea what you're talking about."

"Fine. If you can't be honest with me, then forget it. I don't deserve this." She threw the envelope at him, turned, and strode across the parking lot to her car.

He stared at her as she walked away, at a loss for words. Bending down, he picked up the yellowed envelope. It looked like the one that had fallen out of Seth's yearbook. He'd been so distracted with the prom picture that he'd forgotten about it.

He unfolded the letter. It was addressed to Grace … from Seth.

His hands shook as he read the incriminating words in his best friend's handwriting. Rage flooded through him.

Growling, he kicked the exterior wall of the fire station. How could this be? How could Seth have done this? The fire of anger burned and churned inside him until every cell was ready to burst from the heat. He clenched his fists and fought for control.

Seth had caused Grace emotional and physical hardships that she never should've endured. He'd had so many years to be honest with Grace or to confess to Caleb. All those hours of playing videogames in the barracks or smoking cigars after missions. Seth could've told him the truth. But his best friend had been a coward, never owning up to his actions.

Best friend. The label didn't fit any longer. He was a snake. A fraud.

Caleb crumpled the letter in his hands and threw it on the ground. Now that he knew the truth, it all made sense. Seth discouraging Caleb from asking Grace on a date. Seth's hand almost touching Grace's in the prom picture. Seth's apology before he died.

He clenched his fists so tight that his short nails dug into the palms of his hands. If only Seth were still alive so Caleb could unleash his anger. He'd make Seth explain his actions and give Grace the apology she deserved.

But Seth wasn't here, and the only one who could make this right was Caleb. He had to talk to Grace. After his shift, he would go to the bed-and-breakfast and tell her how he'd found the envelope but never opened it. Hopefully, she would believe him and then, just maybe, she'd let him help her through this.

TWO HOURS LATER, Jennings ran into the room. "Dispatch just called for mutual aid. The Orick Hills Fire Department is already at a fire, and they just got another call." His gaze traveled to Caleb. "Cedar Crest Bed-and-Breakfast is on fire."

The hair on the back of Caleb's neck rose. *Cedar Crest?*

"Suit up. Let's go. No time to waste," Jennings said.

Caleb dashed into the locker room and shoved his gear on as quickly as possible. Had Grace driven to the bed-and-breakfast after she left the fire station? Where was Liam?

After he was dressed, he ran through the firehouse and hopped inside the truck.

In the front seat, Jennings turned on the engine. "Ready?"

Nash nodded. "Ten-four. Let's go."

Caleb bounced his knee up and down as the dispatcher kept them updated. The fire had started on the first floor and now blocked the entrance. It hadn't spread to the second floor or third floor. At least the guests on the second floor had already checked out, but third-floor guests were stuck inside their rooms.

Jennings drove faster.

Caleb's stomach tightened. *Please let Grace and Liam be okay.*

Twenty minutes later, Jennings swerved around the

corner onto Grand Avenue and came to a sudden halt. Bright flames lit the inside of the old mansion like an evil jack-o'-lantern. Dark clouds of smoke spilled out of the roof.

Caleb jumped from the truck as flames broke through the first-story windows and licked the siding. People screamed and pointed to the third floor. A woman leaned out an open window, waving frantically. Her high-pitched screams carried from the open window to the street below.

"Caleb!" Grace's mom sped toward him. Tears streamed down her face, her impassive façade forgotten. "Liam and Davis offered to help clean some of the bedrooms before the fire started. Grace ran in after the boys."

His heart lurched in his chest.

"You have to get them out. I can't lose them." Her lips trembled.

He had to hurry. He circled around the fire truck, and he and Nash maneuvered the ladder toward the window. His heart pounded hard and fast against his chest as he climbed the ladder.

The woman's cries magnified as he neared the window. He stopped at the top of the ladder and extended his arm to her. "I need you to stay calm. One person at a time."

She swung her leg over the windowsill and lunged at

Caleb.

Gripping the ladder with one hand, he held on to her until she found her footing. "You're safe now."

Time seemed to stand still as he helped one person after the next, handing each person to Nash a few feet down the ladder. A heavyset man appeared in the window. "I'm the last one."

Caleb blinked. "The last one? Where are Grace and Liam? Where's Davis?"

The man gave him a frantic look. "I ... I don't know." A mixture of guilt and fear crossed his features.

"I need you to check. Are you sure no one else is in the room with you?"

The man glanced back, then looked at Caleb. "There's no one else here. Get me out. I'm going to faint."

The blood drained from Caleb's face. Where could they be? Was it possible they'd escaped a different way? It didn't seem likely, which meant that they were still inside.

He helped the man out of the window, handed him off to Nash, then spoke into his two-way portable radio. "Did anyone find Grace, her son, or his friend?"

"No one else was found in the basement or first floor," Jennings replied.

"I'm going in, then." Without waiting for confirmation, Caleb heaved himself inside the room. Heat seeped through his uniform as he moved into the hallway. Flames consumed the long, narrow space. He peered through his mask, scanning every inch of the space.

"Grace! Liam!"

No answer.

"Grace!" He walked along the wall, staying as low as possible.

A faint voice came from a nearby room. He ducked inside the room and closed the door. His eyes widened.

Liam was bent over Davis. He glanced up, fear evident in his light green eyes.

"I'm glad you're okay. We need to go."

Liam shook his head. "Davis won't wake up. His arm caught on fire. I put it out right away, and he seemed fine. But when we ran upstairs to escape the fire, he passed out."

"I'll get him. Let's get you two out of here."

Liam didn't budge.

Caleb spoke into his radio, letting the other firefighters know where they were, then he ran to the window and tugged it open.

Nash signaled to their crew, and they moved the ladder to the window.

He quickly scanned the yard as firefighters dashed out the front door. Had they found Grace? He waited for a moment, but only uniformed personnel appeared.

He turned back to Liam. "Have you seen your

mom?"

"No. I thought I heard her once, but I haven't seen her. She's not still in here, is she? You got her out, right?"

Panic seized his insides. He had to find Grace as soon as he helped the boys out. He picked up Davis's limp body.

Nash climbed to the top of the ladder and reached for Davis. He hauled the boy down to the paramedics.

Liam knelt in the same place, unmoving.

He put his hand on Liam's back. "I know you're scared, but we have to go."

"It's not that." Liam tucked his chin to his chest.

"What is it?" He glanced over Liam's shoulder. The flames had crept beneath the closed door and were quickly racing through the room.

"I made a mistake."

"It's okay. We'll talk about it later."

Liam swallowed. "I figured Davis was the one starting the fires, and I didn't tell you."

Davis started the fires? He never would've suspected a kid.

And yet … a memory flooded back to him. A concerned mom with a missing son the night Candy Galore caught on fire. That was why Davis's mom looked familiar at the baseball game. And Davis had been missing because he was the one who started the fire.

He didn't have time for this. They needed to get out

fast. "Come here." He pulled Liam to a standing position, picked him up, and hoisted him out of the window into Nash's arms.

"You need to get out too," Nash said. "The floor could collapse any minute."

"Grace is still in here somewhere."

"It's not safe."

"I'm not leaving until I find her." Squatting low, he opened the door and ran into the hallway. Black heavy smoke blanketed the space. He blinked, then blinked again. He couldn't see. He stopped mid-step as the familiar effects of PTSD trapped his body, and the memory captured his mind.

He peered out the window of the helicopter, squinting through the darkness. Between the zero moon illumination and the dust storm, he could barely see. The ground seemed to blend in with the sky. Which way was up, and which way was down?

He lost control of the aircraft. His stomach did a somersault. He had to regain control. Breathing heavily, he changed the frequency and tightened his grip on the controls. Where was the landing zone?

A faint voiced called from somewhere nearby.

Where was he?

The voice called out again.

He shook his head, shaking away the memory. He wasn't flying. He was inside Grace's bed-in-breakfast.

Grace. Reality washed over him and awakened his senses. He had to find her. He had to get her out of here. He couldn't let her die.

❧

"HELP!" GRACE YELLED above the roar of the fire. "I'm in the bathroom."

No one responded. How long had she been unconscious? Maybe everyone was gone.

After talking to Caleb, she'd taken a long walk to clear her thoughts. As soon as she'd arrived home, she'd seen the smoke. Guests were running outside, screaming. She called 911 just as her mom dashed out to tell her Liam and Davis were still inside. With no firefighters at the scene yet, she couldn't wait. She ran upstairs and began searching room after room.

Before she found the boys, the fire spread to the stairs, blocking her path. She shut the bathroom door, grabbed a towel, and put it under the sink. Pressing the wet, cold cloth against her mouth was the last thing she remembered before she blacked out.

She pounded her fists against the bathroom wall as questions blazed through her brain. Could the firefighters hear her? Would they find her before it was too late? Had they found Liam? Was he safe?

If only she had been at Cedar Crest when the fire

started. She would've gotten Liam out right away.

And she never should've gone to the fire station to confront Caleb. She couldn't let that be their last conversation. She'd been too harsh. She took her shock and anger out on him unfairly. She should've given him a chance to tell his side of the story, but she hadn't let him get a word in. Maybe he'd been waiting to tell her? Had he been unsure of how to do it?

Moisture built in her eyes. She'd made several mistakes. Not just by accusing him, but by not telling him how she felt at the reception.

She'd give anything to go back in time and tell him that she was all in. That she loved him. That she wanted him more than anything. And most of all, that she didn't want to live without him.

Tears streamed down her cheeks. The truth was that she'd been scared of losing him again. And now, he might never know how she felt about him.

She pounded harder on the wall. "Help!"

She pressed the wet cloth against her mouth. Listening. Waiting. Was someone moving toward the bathroom, or was it her imagination? Her pulse pounded in her ears.

A distant voice called from somewhere outside the bathroom. The door swung open, and a rush of smoldering air whooshed into the small space. A firefighter stepped inside and slammed the door shut.

"Grace."

She would recognize Caleb's voice anywhere. A sob escaped through her dry, cracked lips.

In one swift motion, he moved toward her and wrapped his arms around her. "You're alive."

She melted into his embrace. "Oh, Caleb. I'm so glad you heard me. Is Liam okay?"

"Yes."

Relief flooded through her. Her son was safe. She almost passed out again from the rush of emotions and lack of oxygen, but she fought through her foggy brain. In a hoarse voice, she whispered, "I'm so sorry for the way I treated you."

"You need to save your energy." Letting go of her, he spoke into his radio. "Command, this is Engine 22C. I have a victim in the C/D corner of the third floor. I need a ladder to the window now." He waited for a response, then turned his attention to the window. He tried to push it open. "Why isn't this working?"

"The windows are old. They get jammed easily."

He looked around the room. "I need something to break it."

She shook her head. The window was the only way out. She should've bought new windows instead of trying to save money.

"Watch out." Caleb moved across the small room and yanked the shower curtain rod out of place.

She stepped back as he gripped the rod and thrust it at the window. Broken glass shattered to the floor as smoke slithered under the door. Time was running out.

He cleared out the rest of the glass with his glove, then leaned out the window, waving his hands.

He turned around and wrapped her in his arms as thick smoke blanketed the room. "They're coming."

Her lungs burned, and she began to cough uncontrollably.

"You need air." He pulled her close to the window and hoisted her up onto the ledge.

She peered into his helmet. If only she could see his face and look into his sky-blue eyes. Anything to give her comfort in this moment. "Caleb, I lo—"

A loud creaking noise exploded below them. Her ears hummed. She glanced down as the floor collapsed.

Caleb let go of her, and she lost her balance. Before she fell, arms circled around her waist, then her world went black.

Chapter 14

GRACE BLINKED REPEATEDLY and opened her heavily lidded eyes. She looked up at bright fluorescent lights, then closed her eyes again. Pulling the blankets up to her chest, she drifted off to sleep. Images flashed by in her subconscious—reading Seth's letter, searching for Liam, getting stuck in the fire with Caleb.

Her eyes sprung open. *The fire.* She sat up in the bed, her mind racing. She opened her mouth to call out for help, but her throat burned.

Liam shot out of a chair next to the bed. His clothes were wrinkled, and his dark hair was disheveled as if he'd been running his hands through it. "Mom."

She opened her arms, and he climbed into the bed and put his head on her chest. *Her baby.* Thank God he was safe.

Across the room, Amanda stood and walked toward the bed. Dark circles hung beneath her bloodshot eyes. "Let me get you some water." She disappeared from the room for a moment, then returned with a Styrofoam cup. "Drink it slowly. You don't want to throw up."

Grace sipped from the straw, relishing the cold liquid as it soothed her raw throat. "Where's Caleb?" she croaked.

A painful expression pinched Amanda's face. "He's in surgery right now."

"Is he okay?"

Frowning, Amanda glanced at Liam as if trying to decide how much to share. She toyed with the hem of her shirt. "Right as Nash pulled you out of the window, the floor collapsed, and Caleb fell. His legs are broken in several places, and the doctors are checking for possible brain injuries." Her bottom lip trembled. "He's been unconscious ever since the fall."

She tried to process the news, but her body felt numb. "He has to pull through. He has to."

"Yeah. I hope so," Amanda said quietly.

Liam shifted next to her, moving a bandaged hand.

Her eyebrows rose. "Did you get burned?"

He nodded. "I was trying to stop Davis. He was the one who started the fire. He was the one who started the fires in Maple Valley too."

She licked her cracked lips. "Davis was the arsonist?"

"Yeah. He was mad at his mom for wanting to divorce his dad."

"I can't believe it." She took another small sip of water.

"That's why Davis offered to help clean the rooms." With his free hand, Liam ran his fingers along his bandages. "I smelled the smoke and ran into his room, but he'd already lit a bundle of fireworks beneath the bed, and his arm was on fire."

Her eyes widened.

"I knew you kept buckets under the bathroom sinks in case the pipes leaked, so I filled a bucket with water and threw it on his arm." He cuddled closer to her. "I was really scared, but I remembered that Caleb said we can be brave even when we're afraid."

Her chest constricted as she kissed his forehead. "I'm so proud of you."

Two knocks rapped on the door, then Ray stepped inside the room, his face pale and ashen. His gaze traveled to Amanda. "The surgeon wants to talk to us. Caleb just got out of surgery."

Grace sat up straighter. "Is he conscious?"

"The doctor didn't say. We'll let you know as soon as we find out."

She squeezed her eyes shut. *Please wake up, Caleb. I don't want to live without you.*

Chapter 15

G RACE GRIPPED THE steering wheel as she slowly
drove through Orick Hills, toward Cedar Crest.
How much damage had the fire caused? Would she be
able to reopen it?

Part of her didn't want to know the answer. Not yet
anyway. She'd spent the last two days at the hospital, first
recovering from smoke inhalation, then staying in case
Caleb woke up. So far, he was still unconscious.

Guilt pierced her soul. If she hadn't been inside, he
wouldn't have gone in to save her. He'd risked his life for
her. The most selfless thing he could do.

Swallowing hard, she pulled into the parking lot at
Cedar Crest and peered out the windshield.

The charred remains of her bed-and-breakfast looked
more like a bare skeleton than a renovated mansion. One
side of the roof had caved in, leaving the third floor
exposed. Wood blocks crisscrossed over the broken
windows. Yellow warning tape closed off the entrance of
the porch.

She stepped out of her car and cupped a trembling hand over her mouth. How could Davis purposely start a fire at Cedar Crest? Did he consider the damage he would cause? Did he realize the life-altering consequences of his decisions? The people he might hurt?

No, he probably hadn't. He was an angry ten-year-old who wanted to get back at his mom. According to Liam, Davis had started fires at places that meant something to his mom. She worked part-time as a waitress at Candy Galore and Val's Diner. She loved ordering flowers from Fern's Floral. And all of her belongings were at Cedar Crest.

Grace might have felt sorry for him, if not for the destruction he'd caused. At least he'd get the treatment he needed. Jennings had enrolled Davis in the Juvenile Fire-Setting Program. Davis would start participation in the program immediately. Hopefully, it would help him.

She should've listened to Caleb when he'd warned her about Davis. Instead, she'd let her pride and stubbornness get in the way.

She'd done that a lot lately.

Mom parked her car across the street and walked over, her gaze locked on the bed-and-breakfast. Tears spilled over onto her rose-colored cheeks. "I just called the insurance company, and the fire restoration contractor will be here soon."

Grace put her arm around Mom's waist and rested

her head on her mom's shoulder. "Thanks for handling the phone calls."

"Of course."

"If the contractor says it's possible to remodel, do you think we should?"

Mom expelled a heavy breath. "No."

She lifted her head. "What do you want to do, then?"

"I've given this a lot of thought while you were in the hospital." Using her thumb, Mom wiped the mascara trickling down her face. "My sister called yesterday to tell me that the receptionist at the hotel she manages just quit. I could apply for the position. And you loved working at the hospital here. Your license is still valid, and I'm sure they'd take you back, even if it's part-time."

She stepped out of their embrace. "We worked so hard to open Cedar Crest, though."

"Being a good business owner means knowing when to call it quits."

"I agree, but we were only open a year." Grace folded her arms across her chest. "We were learning how to run a business. We can reopen it and start over."

"I appreciate your enthusiasm, but let's face it, we didn't have enough guests."

Grace rubbed her temples. She couldn't argue with that. But could she give up on their dream?

It was all too much. The charred remains of her bed-and-breakfast. Caleb's condition. She knelt on the sidewalk and cupped her hands over her face as tears stream down her cheeks. What would she do if she lost both of them?

⁂

CALEB OPENED HIS eyes. He tried to stretch his arms, but his muscles groaned in protest. In fact, just about everything on his body ached. Where was he? Why was his head throbbing?

He turned his head from side to side, scanning the room. Fluorescent lights. White walls. A nightstand full of cards and flowers. The scent of antiseptic. He was in the hospital.

Fear flowed through the thawed parts of his body that felt like they hadn't moved in days. He lifted his back slightly to rise to his elbows. Two large casts covered his legs. What was wrong with his legs?

A nurse with short gray hair stepped into the room, whistling. She glanced at him, her tune drifting off into silence before she spoke. "You're awake." She walked to his bed, checked the monitors, and put her stethoscope up to his chest. "A strong, steady beat. Good."

Caleb swallowed hard. "Why are my legs in casts?" The question came out slow and strained.

"You broke the femur bone in your left leg, and you broke the tibia bones in both legs." She put two fingers on his wrist. "You'll need physical therapy, but you'll be able to walk again." She smiled. "I'll be back to check on you again soon."

"Wait."

"Yes?"

"Is everyone else from the fire safe? Grace Cunningham? Her son, Liam?"

"Sir, that's confidential information. If she's a patient, I can't tell you. But I can go to the waiting room and see if Grace and Liam are here, though."

"Yes, I'd like that."

As she left the room, Mayor Jennings poked his head inside. His eyes widened. "I wasn't expecting you to be awake."

Wincing, Caleb moved the bed to a slanted sitting position. Not exactly the person he wanted to see right now. Hopefully, the nurse would find Grace.

"I brought this for you." The mayor set a large card on the nightstand. "It's from everyone at the station. We've been taking turns sitting in the waiting room this week while you were unconscious."

Caleb tensed. He'd been unconscious for a whole week?

"You gave us a real scare." Jennings stroked his beard. "You had a lot of nerve to go back in to look for Grace."

"I couldn't let her die," he said slowly.

"I know."

"I should've found her sooner, though."

"What do you mean?"

Caleb glanced down at the wrinkled bedsheets as his groggy mind remembered the events leading to his fall. "My PTSD came back full force. It felt real. I was able to snap out of it when I heard Grace yelling." He lifted his chin. "Until I get it under control, I need to take a leave from the fire department."

Jennings rocked back on his heels. "That's a good choice. In fact, I think this will work out quite well."

He tilted his head to the side. This didn't feel "quite well" to him. And Jennings could at least pretend to be sorry Caleb had to leave the fire department.

The chief placed a hand on Caleb's arm. "You see, I'm not planning on running for mayor again."

His brow furrowed. Where was Jennings going with this?

"*You* would be great. You're confident, hardworking, and intelligent. You care about Maple Valley's citizens, and they love you. All you need is their support. And judging by the full crowd of people out in the waiting room …" The mayor's eyes twinkled. "Well, you got it."

"Mayor. The mayor of Maple Valley." He had to say it aloud. "I've never considered running for an elected position before. Did you not hear the part about PTSD?"

"You'll work that out." Jennings moved his hand to Caleb's shoulder and gave it a gentle squeeze. "Promise me you'll think about it."

He gave a slow nod. "I will."

"I better get going. You have a lot of people out there who will be thrilled to know you're awake."

Before he could consider the mayor's suggestion, footsteps echoed down the hallway. He turned his head as Grace walked inside the room. His lips parted in relief.

Her eyes misted, and a sob escaped through her lips. "You're awake." She rushed across the room, picked up his hand, and laced her fingers between his.

A lump lodged in his throat. Her hair was tied into a messy bun, her shirt was wrinkled, and dark bags hung beneath her eyes. She must've been worried about him.

He rubbed his thumb against her palm. "I'll be honest with you. I wasn't sure we'd make it out in time."

"Me either." She moved to his bed, gently sitting on the edge. "I'm sorry about our last conversation. I should've given you a chance to explain the letter."

His rib cage burned as he moved to his side. "The envelope was in Seth's box of belongings. It must've floated under the bed when I opened his yearbook. I never read it, and I had no idea that Seth had feelings for you."

Seth. Bile rose to the back of his throat. How long would it take before he could talk about Seth without getting angry? Probably a while. The damage Seth caused could never be undone. Hopefully, Caleb would find peace eventually, to let go of the heavy grudge anchored to his chest.

"I shouldn't have accused you." Grace ran her hand through his hair. "I don't want to lose you."

He smiled. "Is that so?"

"Please forgive me for what I'm about to say, but if I don't, I'll regret it for the rest of my life."

"What is it?"

She bit her bottom lip, looking sexier than ever. "While we were in the waiting room this week, I spoke with Mayor Jennings. He told me about the new inn in Maple Valley. My mom and I have decided to own it."

"You were scared to tell me that you're moving to Maple Valley?"

"No. It's what I'm about to say next." She shifted on the bed and met his gaze. "Please stay. I don't want you to leave. I want to give us a chance." A slow, shaky smile spread across her face. "I love you."

His chest filled with warmth. "I love you too."

She leaned over, her face inches away from his. "Does that mean you'll stay?"

"Oh yeah." Caleb wrapped his arms around her, pulling her against him so he could kiss her. So he could show her how much he cared.

He loved Grace now more than he'd ever imagined.

He wouldn't let her get away this time.

꧁꧂

Six months later …

GRACE STOOD ON the porch of the Wildwood River Retreat, holding a giant scissors. A large purple ribbon stretched from one corner of the freshly painted porch to the other. She scanned the crowded lawn—Caleb and Liam, Amanda and Ethan, Ray and Sandy, Charlie and Mac, and many of her new neighbors from Maple Valley waited eagerly. "Ready?"

The crowd shouted with enthusiasm.

She positioned the scissors around the ribbon and smiled. Owning the new inn was a dream come true. Not only would it be a bed-and-breakfast for tourists, but with an additional café and banquet room, it would be the perfect location for wedding events, conferences for groups like Hope for Veterans, and a meeting space for the community committee.

Standing beside Grace, Mom nudged her shoulder. "Let's do this."

Grace nodded and cut the ribbon, then thrust her fist into the air. "The Wildwood River Retreat is officially open!"

The crowd clapped and cheered. Liam jumped up and down. Ray reached for Sandy's hand and kissed her on the cheek. Charlie wrapped his arm around Mac's shoulders. Ethan grinned, then put his hand on Amanda's growing stomach.

Caleb stepped out of the crowd, his gaze resting on Grace. "Before we go inside for the tour, I have something I'd like to say."

The clapping and cheering slowly faded. People near the back stood on their tiptoes to see what Caleb was doing.

Grinning, he walked toward her and pulled a small velvet box out of his pocket. "Grace Cunningham …"

She fanned her face as heat flushed beneath her cheeks.

He knelt down on one knee and opened the box, showcasing a shiny gold band and sparkling diamond. "I've loved you for most of my life. You were my first and only love." He paused for a moment, moisture building in his eyes.

Her chest rose and fell, swelling with emotion.

"You and Liam are my home. You are my lifelong teammate and comrade. I can't imagine a future without you beside me." His Adam's apple bobbed up and down. "Will you marry me?"

She stared at the most handsome man she'd ever laid eyes on and gave several nods before she loudly exclaimed, "Yes!"

Caleb stood and slid the ring on her trembling finger.

She wrapped her arms around his neck as he lifted

her off the ground and spun her in a circle.

The crowd erupted in cheers once again, even louder than before.

He set her on the ground, and Liam ran toward them. Caleb pulled them into a three-way hug.

Her head swam with euphoria. She clutched them close. They were a family now.

Over the top of Liam's head, she kissed Caleb and smiled. The past hadn't been easy, but it had all been worth it.

Author's Note

Dear Reader,

Even though *Stained Heart* is my fifth published book, this was the first novel I ever wrote. I started the first draft when I was in college, and I originally wrote it for a young adult audience. The protagonist, Grace, was eighteen-years-old and she had just discovered she was pregnant. In many ways, the draft was more therapeutic than anything else. I had different experiences than Grace did, but similar enough that I created her character from a very real and personal point of view. After finishing the first draft, I set it aside for almost a decade.

I always knew I'd publish it one day. When I started brainstorming the final book for the *Homebound Series*, I realized *Stained Heart* was the perfect fit. I had so much fun rewriting it as a romance novel and adding in scenes like the helicopter ride, the cave kiss, and my favorite— the accidental date at the bakery.

My dear friends, I hope you enjoyed your last visit to Maple Valley. This fictional town will always have a special place in my heart, and so will its citizens, especially Mac and Charlie, Amanda and Ethan, and Grace and Caleb.

If their love stories touched your heart, brought you to tears, or made you smile, please consider reviewing this series and sharing it with your friends and family.

XOXO,
Crystal

Acknowledgments

I wrote the final draft of this novel in 2020. When the year began, I imagined writing at my favorite coffee shop while my two oldest kids were at school and meeting with my critique partner face-to-face. I couldn't wait to throw a launch party when the book was published. As you can guess, my plans disintegrated before my very eyes. I never would've thought I'd write most of the novel from my home office, aka my kids' play room, aka our preschool and kindergarten school room.

Looking back, it would've been easier to give up and wait for a time when the house was quieter, when toys weren't scattered on the floor by my desk, or little footsteps weren't pitter-pattering upstairs. Oh, yes, it would've been much easier to quit. But I couldn't. Beyond the noise and the mess, I thought of *you*, my readers, and I had to keep going!

I'm beyond grateful to the following people for making this book possible.

My kids—Landon, Zoey, and Savannah—thank you for

letting Mommy write every afternoon. You understood how important this book was to me. You have no idea how grateful I was to spend a little time with my characters each week. I love the three of you so much!

My support group—Mike, Mom and Dad, Lisa and Ben, Jen and Mandie, Sheri and Jenny, thank you for always encouraging me to be the best version of myself as a wife, daughter, sister, friend, and author.

My critique partner—Janice, what would I do without you? You get more and more amazing as the years go by. I'm so excited for your newest adventure to become an editor. Any novelist who decides to hire Lost Canyon Editing is truly blessed!

My research crew—You rock! Eric, Collyn, Callie, and Mayor Gordon, thank you for being so quick to respond to my questions about the air force, firefighting, mayor duties, arsonists, and burns. Your insight helped me create Caleb's character in ways I never could have done on my own. Also, thank you to the Bettendorf Police Department for arranging a meeting with me when I wrote this book as a young adult novel. Your generosity was beyond helpful.

My first and second round of beta readers—Mrs. Coldiron, Mom, Marilyn, Denise, LeeAnn, Kaylee,

Mike, and Jordon, thank you for believing in this book and giving me fabulous feedback.

The Quad City Scribblers—I love connecting with each of you. Your friendships mean so much to me.

Crystal's Crew—thank you for the great brainstorming sessions on our Facebook page. I hope when you read the book, you noticed some of your own ideas.

God—thank you for the internal motivation to finish this book, thank you for my supportive family and friends, and thank you for my amazing readers!

Reader's Guide

1. If you ran into your first love, what would the encounter be like?

2. What are Caleb's stains from the past? What are Grace's stains from the past? How did their past experiences bring them closer?

3. Caleb tells Grace that she deserves to have her tank filled up. Do you know anyone who has an "empty tank?" What can *you* do to fill it?

4. Some people say "time heals all wounds." Do you agree or disagree with this statement?

5. How do Caleb's thoughts about Seth change throughout the novel? How did your thoughts about Seth change?

6. As a single mom, Grace faces many obstacles when it comes to dating. What are some of those obstacles? Why does she open her heart to Caleb?

7. Why is Caleb's decision to reenlist so difficult for him? Who do you turn to when making huge life decisions?

8. The flood in Maple Valley is a major disaster for the town. How does it positively impact Grace, Caleb, and the rest of Maple Valley's citizens by the end? When have you survived difficult circumstances that have brought unexpected blessings?

9. What makes Grace and Caleb good for one another?

10. What is your favorite moment between Grace and Caleb?

Bonus Questions

1. *Shackled Heart*, *Shattered Heart*, and *Stained Heart* are part of the *Homeward Bound Series* because one of the main characters in each novel returns or faces conflicts in their hometown. Why do hometowns elicit a mixture of emotions?

2. If you could visit one "mom and pop" shop in Maple Valley, which one would you choose: Candy Galore, the Canine Palace, Fern's Floral, Charger's Sporting Goods, or the Wildwood River Retreat (Grace's new bed-and-breakfast)?

3. If the characters were real, which couple would you enjoy meeting in person: Mac and Charlie, Amanda and Ethan, or Grace and Caleb?

About the Author

Crystal Joy lives in Iowa with her husband and three growing children. She's a stay-at-home mom with a heart for people. She loves getting to know them, writing about them, and inventing them. When she's not hanging out with the hero and heroine in her latest book, she loves to dance awkwardly, watch reality TV, and visit real locations from her favorite books.

You can learn more about Crystal Joy at her website crystaljoybooks.com.

Made in the USA
Columbia, SC
28 January 2024